BRYONY ROSEHURST

Cursed in Love

Contents

Content Warnings

Luce suffers from anxiety and depression, and her medication is mentioned. On-page anxiety attacks.

Mild violence and language.

Mentions of illness, death, and grief.

Chapter One

Luce had been hoping for a spa — one of those fancy ones in a grand manor that always smelled like lemons or cucumber, with complimentary prosecco offered as you walked through the door. Somewhere idyllic and rural, but not out of range of a 4G signal, and preferably with no cow pat on the ground. She'd been looking forward to fluffy, white bathrobes and hand massages, facials and bubble baths that would shed away her old skin and leave her silky and new. When her best friend — only friend, really — and coworker, Juliet, had practically forced her out of the office for the first time since she'd been hired by the law firm three years ago, gifting her a holiday booking as a late-Christmas-slash-early-birthday-present, a nice little spa break was exactly what Luce had pictured. Juliet was classy like her. They drank margaritas on a Friday night and bought all of their blazers from Selfridges.

So why on God's green earth was Luce pulling up to a cluster of damp, rustic cabins in the middle of the Scottish Highlands rather than a pretty, little countryside estate?

Had her sat-nav malfunctioned?

The weathered wooden sign that greeted her read *Alasdair Ridge*, complete with a painted set of mountains and… oh, heavens… a bloody kayak.

Luce turned off the engine and glared at the endless, tall trees and dreary, gray sky through her rain-speckled windshield. She had taken this break because Juliet promised that she would love it. *You need to relax, Luce. Have a week to yourself!*

How was Luce supposed to bloody relax when her tires were currently being swallowed by marshy soil? Did Juliet know her at all?

No. This had to be a mistake. Luce whipped her phone from her purse on the passenger seat beside her and scrolled through her contacts with a huff. When she tried to dial Juliet, though, she realized that the bars that usually displayed her mobile data in the top corner of her screen were nonexistent. No 4G to be found, or even 3G. She would even put up with 2G if need be, though she wasn't sure it existed anymore.

She had no choice but to stomp out of the car, groaning when her brand-new Chelsea boots squelched in an ankle-deep puddle. Around her, families bustled to and from their cars, carrying tents and sleeping bags and wearing — even the word made her shudder, God help her — *gilets*.

Cringing, Luce did her best to escape the mud, hopping toward the wooden porch of a small lodge labeled *Reception*. The drizzling, wintry rain speckled her cheeks and dampened her hair, and she hauled up the furry hood of her coat to protect herself as she waited for any sign of life on her phone.

Finally, after an eternity, a 3G sign appeared. Luce breathed a sigh of relief and called Juliet again, pinning the phone to her already frostbitten ear. As the ringing tone droned, she jiggled her knees to get the blood flowing in her legs again. A seven-hour drive in stiff denim jeans had done her circulation no good at all.

"Hello?" Juliet chirped finally on the other end of the line. From the tinniness of her voice and the whirring engine in the background, Luce suspected that she was driving — probably home from work, given the time. Luce should have been doing the same thing. She *wished* she was.

"Tell me I'm in the wrong place," Luce begged, crossing her arms against a sudden cold wind.

"Did you follow the directions I sent?"

"Yes." Luce gritted her teeth.

"And are you on the Isle of Skye?"

"It certainly would seem that way, yes."

"Alasdair Ridge?"

Luce scowled at the welcome sign again. "Mm-hmm."

"Then you're in the right place, my love." She could practically hear Juliet's dazzling grin seeping through her words — much in the same way that the rain was seeping through Luce's boots.

"Don't 'my love' me, you sneaky so-and-so. I thought I was going somewhere nice! Why would you send me *here*?" Luce kept her words to a whisper-shout on account of the family passing by.

"It *is* nice!" Juliet argued with what was either a tut or the tick of her indicator. "You need to learn to be at one with nature, Luce. You're always in the office. When was the last time you saw *grass*?"

"I don't need to see grass. I have *carpet* and shiny wooden floors. They keep my feet clean and dry and warm, and cows don't try to eat them."

"Look, the hubby and I" — Luce rolled her eyes; she hated

3

it when Juliet called her husband "the hubby" unironically — "*loved* Alasdair Ridge. Saved our marriage, you know. And our sex life."

Luce went from rolling her eyes to trying to staunch her gag reflex. "Please warn me before you start talking about sex. My day is bad enough as it is. I don't want to think about you and Keith rolling about in the mud."

"Oh, I do apologize, Your Holiness. I suppose your involuntary celibacy makes it difficult to hear about S-E-X."

Anger curdled in Luce's gut. Her complete lack of intimacy was entirely voluntary. She didn't have any spare time or energy to pour into another person, and what was wrong with that? Her vibrators did it better, anyway, and they didn't ask for anything more afterward. "Piss off."

"I'm just saying," Juliet continued, "I think this will be good for you. Just because you don't want it doesn't mean you don't *need* it. I've watched you work your arse off day in, day out for three years now, and while I admire you for it… bloody hell, you need to chill the fuck out, babes. You'll have a heart attack by the time you hit thirty if you're not careful, and then I'll have to deal with Val's tyranny all on my own."

Val was their haughty, unpleasant boss, and loved to remind them both of such at any opportunity she got. If Luce made one typo in her paperwork or stumbled a little bit in her closing speech, Val was always there, watching, waiting for the moment to slip it into casual conversation as a snide remark or a way of belittling her.

"And please tell me how climbing trees and getting pissed-wet through in a dirty cabin will help me chill the fuck out," Luce said, eyeing the tall pines again. She noticed now that some of them were surrounded by platforms, with zip wires and bridges knitted throughout the forest. It wasn't just a place to camp or hole up in a tiny cabin but also a place to wear tight harnesses and helmets that probably still smelled of the stale sweat and rancid fear of their last owner. Luce knew what to expect from one too many school trips as a teenager, all of which her mother had forced her on to keep her "well-rounded." Now here she was again. It was almost as though nothing had changed. Just once, she would like to be forced on a bloody all-inclusive trip to Mallorca or the Maldives.

"You don't have to do that stuff," Juliet said. "You can sign up for their outdoor yoga classes... or go hiking... ooh, and we really enjoyed the canoeing!"

Luce had never touched a canoe in her life and had no desire to now. Did her supposed best friend not know her at all? What had Luce done to deserve *this*? "That's it. I'm coming home."

"You're bloody well not! I paid for this trip. You will enjoy it!"

"You only got it because of a Wowcher coupon!" Luce pointed out. It was only a guess, of course, but Juliet tended to get most of her things from coupon websites, whether it was Keith's Christmas socks, cat food, or her annual holiday to Skegness.

"I don't care. It still cost money. Besides, you never do anything fun with that stick up your arse! I did something nice for you because I care, and you're *going* to enjoy it. Please just check in and enjoy my gift. And bring me back some Scottish shortbread!"

The line went dead before Luce could protest again, and she shook her head in exasperation. This was the last time she ever accepted a gift from anyone.

Still, a shred of guilt niggled at her. She didn't mean to be ungrateful. She just didn't want to spend a rare week off soggy and cold and miserable. It was kind of Juliet to worry about Luce's well-being, but... there was no need. She was only a *little* bit stressed. She only ground her teeth in her sleep every night and woke with an aching jaw every morning. She only got heart palpitations now and again and lived off a constant supply of coffee, which did not mix very well with her perpetual anxiety and antidepressants.

Luce slumped, defeated. She *did* need a break, and this appeared to be as good as she was going to get. Warily, she wandered into the reception and prayed that nobody would force her into a helmet and harness.

She would draw the line at those.

Chapter Two

It was a cold and miserable day, and Ophelia was quite ready to close up the museum and have it done with. In fact, she had placed down her mug of tasteless, sachet-made hot chocolate and was about to change the *Open* sign to *Closed* at the door when two men walked in, shaking raindrops from their umbrellas. The tails of their long coats and leather shoes dripped, water puddling on the tired welcome mat and slipping through the creaky floorboards. Ophelia suppressed a sigh. Now she would have to mop up for the fifth time that day.

Except one of the men was familiar: the eldest, silver-haired and chiseled. Leonard Green had been her mentor back when she'd been studying for a master's degree in archaeology. A fat lot of good that did for her in the end. Other than stumbling across a few new fossils along Skye's coastline, she hadn't worked anywhere remotely interesting in well over a year. Then again, that was probably her own fault.

"Leonard!" Ophelia greeted him with a toothy smile. "What

a pleasant surprise!"

Leonard slipped off his glasses to wipe the rain-spattered lenses with a handkerchief, his eyes widening with recognition. "Oh, hello! I didn't recognize you for a moment! What are you doing in old Farnoch?"

"I work here now." Ophelia tugged at the hem of her pleated skirt and adjusted her collar, suddenly aware of the other pair of eyes on her. His companion was craggy-faced, chin dusted with stubble, his dark eyes watching her carefully. "It's quiet, but… there's history here if you know where to find it." Which, at present, she didn't, though she didn't dare say so.

"As with anywhere. Good for you, Ophelia. It's always nice to see a student continuing one's career after study." Leonard glanced around, scratching his cleft chin and pushing his round-framed glasses back onto the smooth bridge of his nose. "How rude of me. This is a, er, friend from the university. Hector. He's interested in a few pieces you've got here and proposed we venture out to see them in person."

"It's nice to meet you." Ophelia nodded politely, and Hector returned the gesture. Still, his rugged features remained blank, sharing none of Leonard's warmth or friendliness, and it left Ophelia shifting on her feet uncomfortably. "Any exhibits in particular you'd like to see?"

Hector clutched his gloved hands behind his back and began to wander the space, perusing the artifacts on show. Many of them had been found and preserved well before Ophelia's time, though she'd had a hand in locating others. "Do you find a lot of fossils around these parts?"

"Not as many as you would along the coast." Ophelia motioned him toward a display of fossils cordoned off with rope along the back wall. Her heels clicked in the thick silence, accompanied by the shuffling of Hector following behind. "We have plenty of Jurassic ammonites, of course, though they're common enough that I doubt you came all the way here for them."

Hector inspected them with little interest. "For such a small village, the collection is impressive."

"To tell you the truth," Leonard chimed in, "I saw something about a few relics on your website. A ring, was it?"

Ophelia's heart stuttered, a pang of dread forcing its way through her. Of course they would have to be here for the one exhibit she could no longer even bring herself to look at. The one that had caused her so much pain, so much loss, since she had recovered it from the lake pooling between the hilly lands just north of here.

"Eilidh's ring?" she asked. Even the name tasted bitter on her tongue.

Leonard's face brightened. "That's the one! Is it still here, by any chance?"

With an unenthusiastic nod, Ophelia led them over to its podium, where it hid behind a glass casement mirroring their faces. The two men crowded around her as she tried not to catch the eye of the sapphire embedded in the band. It always seemed to be watching her, that rich-blue, wicked stone. "I recovered this one myself from a lake in the mountains."

"It's magnificent. Whereabouts was it found?" Leonard asked.

"Not far from a remote hamlet in the Cuillin mountain range, named High Mór. I came across it by chance, actually. I'd heard about Eilidh's story before, of course, but I never expected to find the ring myself — or, at least, a ring remarkably similar." And how she wished she hadn't. But she'd come across Eilidh's lake, labeled by a corroding, powdery headstone, and hadn't

9

been able to help herself. She was an archaeologist first, after all, and an avid lover of history. If there was something she could find to validate the truth of what was believed by many in Skye to be a mere old wives' tale, she wanted to find it.

"I read the story online," Hector said, indicating the plaque detailing Eilidh's famous story. "It's remarkable. What makes you sure the ring is truly hers?"

"We'll never be sure," Ophelia admitted. "But it was found at the supposed site of Eilidh's death. If it isn't hers, it's certainly a wonderful coincidence. It's described with the same sapphire in the stories."

"A Hebridean sapphire?"

Ophelia nodded.

"We wouldn't be able to examine it more closely, would we?" Leonard questioned, taking off his glasses again to chew on the temple tips.

Ophelia couldn't help but shudder, goosebumps pimpling her arms beneath the frilly sleeves of her blouse. "I'm afraid not. I wouldn't wish that upon anyone."

"Why not?" Hector narrowed his eyes.

"Well, if you've read the story, you know about the curse."

The men blinked blankly at Ophelia for a moment. It was Hector who laughed first, a trapped snort escaping from him as he adjusted his leather gloves. "You can't seriously believe that the ring is cursed. It's just a fable meant to scare women away from trusting their men."

"I thought the same," Ophelia whispered, "until I found Eilidh's ring. Now everybody who's seen it believes the story was real, that Eilidh truly existed, and this is the proof. And *I* was the one to disturb it. I touched the ring, and I wound up… cursed."

"Ophelia...." Leonard sighed sympathetically, squeezing Ophelia's shoulder gently. "I doubt you could ever be cursed. I'm certain that whatever happened, it's only coincidence."

Ophelia welled with frustration, with raw pain. She *was* cursed, and she'd hoped that maybe Leonard was experienced enough to be able to help her. "You've never worked with a cursed relic before?"

It was Hector who tapped the glass at the center of the ring, his brows rising into his receding hairline. "I've heard Hebridean sapphire can absorb all sorts of karma and luck — and pass it on, I'd imagine. I've worked with cursed relics before, plenty of times... and believe it or not, the strongest mystical energy usually begins with a Hebridean sapphire."

She loosed a sharp breath — of relief or desperation, she wasn't quite sure, but she had to restrain herself from clawing Hector's arm and begging him for a way to break the curse, to get her life back. "Do you know anything more? Is there a way to reverse a curse?"

Hector shrugged, tucking his hands into his pockets. His pale-blue eyes danced with something indecipherable.

Ophelia's attention flickered to Leonard desperately, but his own remained steady on Hector. "I'm no expert in mystical matters, but I have heard of ways to lift curses from relics."

"How?" She was one moment away from getting down on her knees and begging.

"Well," Leonard started, "it usually involves returning the object to the place it belongs. I suppose in Eilidh's eyes, you stole something from her. You took the ring from its resting place, and from hers. Your best bet would be putting it back, where the curse can't find you anymore."

Ophelia's brows knitted together, and she staggered back as

though an invisible wind had shoved her. Hope flickered like a candle in her gut for the first time since all of this had begun. She had a solution, or at least an idea of one. She might finally be free. "Of course. Why hadn't I thought of that?"

"Why don't we sit down and talk about this properly?" Leonard proposed. "I don't suppose there's any chance of a hot cuppa, is there?"

With her lack of visitors today and the newly opened café across the road, Ophelia had tucked away Morag's kettle in the back. She nodded, still absently mulling over Leonard's idea. "Is tea okay for you both?"

"Perfect," said Hector with a grin.

Ophelia wandered behind the front desk and into the back corridor, shivering as she stepped into the cool kitchen. The afternoon was gloomy behind the old lace curtains, and she switched on the light before filling the kettle and leaving it to boil.

Her mind was still on the ring, on returning it. She'd have to go alone, of course, and Morag, the museum's owner, wouldn't just let her take a relic from her exhibition. How could Ophelia get it out and back into the lake, then? She couldn't very well just *steal* it... could she?

If it ended this godforsaken curse, the long line of terrible dates and all of the days she spent alone, she'd do anything. The only problem was that she didn't want to exchange her dire luck for a criminal record. If she disappeared with the ring, she'd be the number-one suspect, and it would be a few days' trek off any beaten path to get to the lake. Perhaps she could explain things to Morag. Morag was kind and warm and had been there through Ophelia's darkest times — ones she now blamed on the curse. Maybe Morag would understand and let her take the ring.

Absently, she twirled her own band around the fourth finger of her left hand, a habit she had formed long before the curse began. The kettle whistled to a boil as she finally snapped out of her schemes of heists and going on the run, retrieving two chipped teacups from the small cupboard and then her own tea-ring-stained mug from the side.

She opened the tea bag tin and found it empty.

With a sigh, Ophelia stepped back into the corridor to tell her visitors the terrible news — but their hushed voices stopped her cold.

"We'll take it now. You can talk her out of reporting it. Tell her your sad little tale."

It was Hector who spoke, the gravelly words whispered conspiratorially.

"We don't have a key," Leonard responded. Ophelia frowned. Quietly, she shuffled further down the corridor and peered around the slightly open door to see what was going on. Her mentor and his friend still stood around Eilidh's ring.

"Then ask her for it." Hector clenched his jaw, a threat glinting in his eyes.

Leonard scraped a hand roughly across his face, appearing suddenly tired — haggard, even — his hair mussed and his face wrinkled with lines Ophelia hadn't noticed before. "She won't let me just take a relic, especially not if she thinks it's left her cursed."

"If she's stupid enough to believe in curses, I'm sure we can convince her one way or another. But if you'd rather do it the hard way…" Without warning, Hector smashed a gloved hand through the protective glass. Fragments rained down onto the floor, and Ophelia startled against the shattering sound. Her pulse pounded in her ears as she searched desperately for a way to stop them — two relatively tall, broad men against her.

And her mentor. A man she had looked up to and respected and trusted, and he was trying to steal from her. Why?

All Ophelia knew was that she couldn't just let the ring go. She had to break the curse first.

Without thinking, she raced back down the corridor and swiped a serrated knife from the small collection above Morag's rusty old hob — which she technically wasn't insured to use, though she baked the occasional biscuits or made hot sandwiches and soup, asking the locals to keep it a secret.

Ophelia's hand shook with the weight of the knife's hilt, but the weight of the curse was so much heavier, so much more stifling, and she was so tired of living with it every day. This was the only opportunity she would get to stop it. She could blame the missing ring on Leonard and his pet thief.

She sprinted back into the gallery, extending the kitchen knife in front of her with more courage than she felt. "Put the ring down. Now."

The men lifted their heads, pinning Ophelia with their eyes. Leonard's eyes swam with guilt, but Hector's lip curled with determination as he clutched the ring in his gloved hand unwaveringly.

"Put it *down*! I mean it. I'm a furious woman with a kitchen knife!" Ophelia dared a step forward. Her gaze whipped to Leonard accusingly. "You lied to me. Why?"

"I… I'm sorry. I truly am," Leonard stuttered out. Ophelia hated herself for believing him.

"Why? Why do you want the ring?"

Hector smirked. "Hebridean sapphire isn't only useful for its curses, love. It's incredibly rare and incredibly valuable, too."

Chapter Two

"So — what? You're a con man? A thief?" Ophelia surmised, her voice breathy with incredulity.

Hector only shrugged as though the conclusion was a fair one and held out his hand. Eilidh's ring winked against the ceiling lights, a smooth, wicked deep blue.

"Tell you what," Leonard broke in. "I'll cut you into the deal if you show us where you found this."

Ophelia's lips parted in surprise, and she looked to Leonard as though he were still her mentor, as though he might help her. He didn't. He remained looking vaguely concerned and irritatingly sympathetic, his brow furrowed.

"That wasn't what we discussed," Hector ground out.

"She could prove useful. Who's to say there isn't more sapphire in that little lake she found?"

If there was, Ophelia hadn't seen it, and she would never be compelled to fulfill someone else's plain greed. Still, she kept her mouth shut, eyeing the ring once more. She needed to break the curse, and it was there, calling to her, no longer any glass to keep her away. It could prove a blessing or just another curse.

Things couldn't get any worse either way.

Swinging her leg into Hector's extended arm, Ophelia silently thanked her mother for all of those self-defence and karate classes she'd been forced to take before her exchange year abroad in Italy.

The ring dropped to the floor, and Ophelia wasted no time in retrieving it from the broken glass, closing her fist around it until shards of glass splintered her palms as she fled from the museum. She didn't care. She had the ring and an idea of how to lift the curse, if Leonard had at least been honest about that.

Now she just had to get rid of the men chasing after her.

Luckily, she also had a car, old and tired as it was, and after dropping the knife she yanked her keys from the pocket of her skirt to unlock it. When she glanced over her shoulder, two shadows darkened her vision. She didn't give them time to blacken it completely, thrusting her keys into the ignition and thanking the heavens that it started on the first attempt — for once — though the exhaust did let out a thick plume of smoke as she roared off.

She took a final glance at Leonard, flanked by the con man, in the wing mirror, another slice of anger — betrayal — cutting through her. Then again, perhaps she should have thanked him for making it so easy.

The only problem was that she knew they would follow. Hector had been intense, intimidating, in his determination and greed. The fact left her no time to do anything but speed her way to Alasdair Ridge and hope that they didn't reach the trail toward High Mór before she did.

Chapter Three

nger still simmered beneath Luce's skin an hour after she had checked in at the front desk. It wasn't because she'd been tricked into coming here, or even because there were slug trails on the welcome mat of her cabin. In fact, other than the pests it wasn't so bad at all, with a log fire guttering in the corner and a comfortable mattress piled high with blankets.

No, it was Juliet's words that had riled Luce, though it had taken her a while to come to that realization. *You never do anything fun with that stick up your arse.*

It was true that Luce wasn't much of an adventurer. She had always been the sensible friend, the designated driver, the leader of the group project, always focused on getting where she wanted to be. She hadn't always wanted to be so uptight, but… it was difficult not to be with her heart always pounding so violently in her chest. She needed the soft security of her comfort zone at all times, and that meant she needed a steady career and a daily structure, needed to know what was about to come next at any given time, because one unpredicted event might send her into a spiral that could take months to adjust to.

So, no, she didn't do anything fun, because fun wasn't *fun* for her. Fun was stressful and exhausting and stomach-churning. Fun was pretending to be somebody she just couldn't be, somebody her mind and body wouldn't *let* her be. But now she was in a bloody cabin in the middle of nowhere, with nobody she knew nearby, and if she sat down on that tattered, old couch with nothing to concentrate on but the peeling paint on the walls, she might actually go mad. The only way she normally kept her anxiety in check was by focusing on work or, on the weekends, distracting herself with household chores and visits to her mum's house.

Coming here had been a big, big mistake, and the unfamiliar walls of the cabin were swiftly beginning to press in on her. She'd already unpacked her suitcase and had nothing left to focus on but the heavy silence.

After swallowing down two beta-blockers with tepid water from the tap, Luce slung her thick coat back on and headed out again, glad to find that it had at least stopped drizzling. The heady smell of damp earth and what was probably animal urine followed her back to the reception building, soil and soggy leaves sticking to the soles of her boots in clumps.

The young blond-haired woman who had checked her in an hour ago still stood at the front desk, playing a game of solitaire on the computer without any sort of subtlety. She looked up as Luce approached. "Back so soon?"

Luce forced a smile. "I was wondering if there are any villages nearby. Not the one I passed through to get here, but maybe something... with more to do." The small village she'd passed through, Farnoch, was obnoxiously quaint and touristy, and Luce hadn't spotted anything interesting save for a couple of soap shops, a sad-looking museum, and a chippy.

"Well, there's Loch Brittle, which is only a wee drive from here—"

Luce couldn't do a bloody loch. She'd seen five on the way here, and they were all just a lot of water and hills mostly hidden by gloomy clouds. "I was thinking of a nice restaurant or... I don't know, just something to keep me occupied. Preferably somewhere with Wi-Fi."

The receptionist looked at Luce as though she had grown a second head, her forehead wrinkling. "If you're looking for something to keep you occupied, ma'am, there's no better place for you than here. We have a range of activities available." A leaflet was shoved toward her — the same one that had already been given to her upon arrival. Luce had perused it in five minutes and concluded that Juliet could not have chosen a worse place for her.

She opened her mouth to tell the receptionist as much, but Juliet's words echoed in her mind again. *You never do anything fun with that stick up your arse.*

Was she really going to go and find an internet café somewhere so that she could get back to *work*? Couldn't she at least *try* to be a normal, adventurous, interesting human being? She was in the Highlands, after all. All alone, with no pressure but that of her own mind.

Was this who she wanted to be when she was free?

With a sigh, she skimmed through the pamphlet as though she might find something different in it this time around. "All right. What would you recommend for a perpetually anxious workaholic who doesn't want to be here?"

"Er..." The receptionist bit her lip. "Honestly? You'll probably hate most of these things — but everybody who comes here loves taking a canoe onto the river. You can choose between the calm waters or head toward Alasdair Falls. It's free to hire for our cabin guests, too."

Even the thought of paddling around in a canoe alone like the glossy people photographed in the pamphlet made Luce feel nauseous. Once, her mother had forced her onto a Caribbean cruise ship for two weeks and she'd spent the entire time vomiting — not from seasickness but from irrational worries about the ship sinking or contracting an exotic virus or accidentally falling overboard. Her mind had become the most terrifying place on earth, and it was the one thing she couldn't escape. "What if I drown?"

The receptionist gave a soft, pitying smile. "You won't. You'll be wearing a life vest, and our canoes are very sturdy, very safe. Besides, the calmer waters for our beginners are shallow."

Defeated, Luce slumped. "All right. Fine. But I should warn you that I'm a lawyer, and that means that if I do drown, you'll be getting sued."

The receptionist had the good sense to widen her eyes in alarm. "Noted, ma'am. I'll, er, help you find the canoes, shall I?"

Luce rolled her eyes and nodded, her palms already growing clammy. "I suppose you'd better, before I change my mind."

* * *

"Just remember to take the right side when you reach the fork in the river." The receptionist, whose name Luce had learned was Alex, pointed down the river as Luce steadied herself in her canoe, her inflated life vest puffing her chest up until she couldn't see her waist — or her hands, which were now clutching a wooden paddle. "And keep an eye on the time. It will be getting dark in a couple of hours."

It was already dark and had been all day. British winters sucked all the color from the world, and Luce had been waiting desperately for a sign of spring. There was none yet, other than the temperature rising to an impressive six degrees celsius, according to her car thermometer this morning. "Are you sure I don't need training or something? I mean, I've never done this — oh!"

Alex pushed the canoe off the riverbank before Luce could finish her sentence, leaving her to float forward in the subdued current. As Luce craned her neck to look over her shoulder, Alex waved. "Bye! Have fun!"

"I'm a lawyer!" Luce reminded her, though her words were lost to the wind and Alex was already heading back toward the cabins. The biting cold was a harsh reminder of how badly she didn't want to do this, and with panic wriggling through her gut, Luce swallowed and tried to steer herself back to the banks. Her teeth chattered audibly above the burbling current, her biceps burning as she pushed.

"Oh, thank God," she breathed when she caught sight of somebody running toward her as she reached the bank: another woman, this one closer to Luce's age, with tousled, rust-tinted hair and rosy cheeks. "Excuse me!" she called. "I've made a huge mistake and I need help getting back on dry land!"

If the woman heard her, she didn't show it. She was still sprinting. A ways behind her, Luce glimpsed the shadows of two others following, running equally fast. Was she being *chased*?

Luce didn't want to find out. She had problems of her own to contend with. Frowning, she tried to steady the boat against the bank with her paddle, but she couldn't find the coordination in her jerky motions to accomplish much of anything.

"I'm terribly sorry, miss, but I'm afraid I have to commandeer this canoe," the woman said breathlessly as she reached Luce. She hopped straight from the riverbank into the canoe with more grace than Luce had on solid ground, sending the boat — and them — swaying roughly.

"Wait, what?" Luce stuttered as the second paddle was snatched from where it lay at her feet. The woman sat on the bench in front of Luce and began to paddle, her long pleated skirt fanning out beneath her as she glanced back at her pursuers, who were nearing: two middle-aged men, their faces set with determined, harsh lines. What on earth had she done to warrant being chased by them? And what had Luce done to warrant being dragged into whatever mess this was? "Let me go!" she ordered when her senses slowly began to return. "I want to get off!"

"I'm sorry, miss, I really am." The woman — the canoe hijacker — at least had the decency to wince apologetically over her shoulder, her nose runny and pink from the cold. "It's a matter of emergency."

She paddled faster, the current dragging the canoe effortlessly downstream. Though the waters were calm, Luce's stomach swooped, and she clutched the splintered bench for dear life. She needed control. She was *always* in control. How had it been taken from her so easily now?

"I don't bloody care what it is!" she exploded. "Let me off this canoe *now*!"

"I can't do that. They're chasing me."

The breeze whipped through Luce's hair, peeling her skin off with its claws and leaving her raw.

"Who are they?" She looked back again, fear tightening like a fist in her chest. They were almost at the edge of the riverbank, but the canoe was slipping quickly away and there was no way of them catching up now through the thick underbrush lining this section of the river.

"I'll explain everything, I swear. Just…"

"*Wait!*" Luce screamed as they neared a fork in the river, remembering Alex's words. They had to go right.

But the woman was steering left.

"No! This isn't the right way!"

It was too late. The waters grew choppy as they dropped into the left fork, bumping over jutting rocks and catching the last of winter's dying leaves in the boat. Luce held on to the bench so tightly that her palms stung and her knuckles turned white, and she couldn't keep her eyes open when they dropped once, twice, three times, down a series of small dips and falls.

"I'm a lawyer!" she warned, scrunching her eyes closed. "I could sue you!"

"Sorry!" was the woman's only reply. In the grand scheme of things, the word held little weight — especially since they were swiftly hurtling down the river now, toward the foaming edge of a waterfall.

Luce's screech was earsplitting as they dropped all at once, the world torn from beneath them. When they roughly settled into the water again, she expected that to be the end of it, but she didn't even have the chance to breathe a sigh of relief before they were falling again, icy water dampening Luce's hair, her jeans.

"Sorry!" the woman repeated.

"You will be!" Her warning was lost to another drop, this one lasting so long that Luce couldn't remember a world wherein she was not dropping off the earth. She had always been here, suspended and cold and afraid, her organs somersaulting and rearranging themselves. *This* was her world forever: clutching on to nothing as she was tugged into turbulent waters. And then drowning.

She was drowning as she landed with the canoe no longer beneath her. Foul-tasting water flooded her mouth as the current dragged her down with merciless determination. She kicked, her screams stifled and unending until finally, there, a shimmer of light. The surface. She reached for it desperately, breaking through the waves and heaving, choking, still somewhere between breathing and drowning. She clutched an overhanging tree branch for dear life, her entire body somehow both numb and more awake than it had ever been before. Her life vest seemed to work too late, leaving her to float and bob unsteadily.

A flash of blue alerted her to the capsized canoe floating past, still carried along by falls and the current. Luce searched for the woman, her veins buzzing with adrenaline and dread. She found her not too far away, hauling herself up a fallen tree trunk on the same side of the river. She froze as she caught Luce's eye.

And then she *waved*.

Luce was going to kill her if she ever figured out how to get out of this alive. As it was, she was still clinging onto the branch, her arms searing with a tension she didn't dare lose. If she let go, even for a moment, she'd be lost to the water again. Nearly drowning had been so much worse than her catastrophizing had ever made it out to be, and she never wanted to feel that resistance, that entrapment, again. Still, her anger was worse, and she flipped the woman her middle finger before shimmying down the branch and onto the bank. Her damp clothes dragged her down and her limbs had stiffened to blocks of ice, but somehow, finally, she collapsed onto marshy mud — and screamed until her voice echoed off the surrounding trees and mountains.

Chapter Four

Perhaps Ophelia had made a small error in judgment in commandeering the stranger's canoe. Tiny, really. How was she to know they'd end up caught in a current and hurtling down seven-foot waterfalls? She'd just been so desperate to lift the curse that she'd hopped onto the river without thinking twice, hoping Leonard and Hector couldn't follow.

At least now she was headed in the right direction to High Mór. She would just have to do some damage control first.

The brunette canoer was already on the riverbank by the time Ophelia made it across the fallen tree trunk and onto dry land. Needless to say, the canoe itself was long gone, and perhaps the stranger's sanity with it. She was currently glowering at Ophelia with a bitterness that would put lemons to shame, and Ophelia winced and smiled uncomfortably.

"I think we might have gotten off on the wrong foot."

"The wrong foot?" the woman repeated incredulously, swiping her damp hair from her slitted eyes. Dead leaves clung to her, gathering in the crevices of her life jacket, and dirt speckled her face. Her irises were a piercing green, her features lined thinly with rage. "I could have *drowned!*"

"You're wearing a life jacket," Ophelia pointed out quite reasonably, though not unapologetically.

"I don't *care!*" The woman's voice ricocheted off the trees like gunfire. "Maybe I just fancied a calm canoe along the river! Maybe I didn't want to be thrown from three waterfalls because a stranger hijacked my peaceful holiday!"

Through her words, Ophelia noticed her teeth chattering, and it reminded her of just how freezing she was. Her soggy tweed dress weighed down her bones and chafed her skin, her hands numb from cold. How she would survive another couple of days in these clothes, she didn't know — but going back wasn't an option now. It was only a matter of time before they would be back on her tail, if they were as determined to get the ring as they'd seemed in the museum.

The ring.

Fear lanced through Ophelia at the realization that it had been tucked into her coat pocket and might have fallen out. It would be typical of her to lose Eilidh's ring and end up cursed for the rest of her life.

She rooted quickly to find out her fate, breathless and panicked and —

The rough Hebridean stone fell into her hand, the smooth silver band cool in her prune-like palm. "Oh, thank God."

"Oh, I'm sorry, am I keeping you from something more important? Did you perhaps find a set of car keys you might have used instead of my bloody *canoe?*" the woman seethed.

Ophelia grimaced, her relief making room for guilt, too. "I'm sorry. I really am. If you'd just let me explain..."

"Oh, you're going to explain. But first, you're going to take me back to my cabin, where I can call the police!"

Brows knitting together, Ophelia glanced at the rocks jutting over them on every side. In this condition, soggy and recovering from shock, they wouldn't make it back up the hills to Alasdair Ridge. Even if they weren't in such a state, it was a steep hike unless they could find the road again, which could be far from the river at this point. They needed to get warm before they tried to do anything. They needed a fire.

"We won't make it back unless you're a skilled rock-climber. How about we get warm first, and then I can tell you my side of things?"

"Oh, yes, let's get warm. Good idea," the stranger spat. "Only we're *soaking* wet *outside* in the middle of *winter*."

"I can make us a fire, but we need to get away from the riverbank in case Leonard finds us."

"Who the fuck is Leonard?"

"One of those men you saw chasing after me. Look, it's a long story and I know this must be confusing for you, but... please." It was a desperate plea. Ophelia needed the curse lifted. She needed to get to High Mór. She couldn't do any of it if this woman stopped her now — though of course, she had every right to.

The woman looked her up and down, her gaze scathing and icier than the river they'd just emerged from. "Are you some sort of criminal?"

"No. *They're* the criminals." It shouldn't have felt like a lie, but it was becoming one the longer she carried the ring.

"Why? Who are they?" She narrowed her eyes, burying her pointy chin in her life vest as she shivered. "I'm a lawyer. I can give you legal advice."

Oh, bollocks. The law had already caught up to Ophelia. What would a lawyer make of her stealing a ring from the museum? She supposed that if she were a defense lawyer it wouldn't matter, as long as she was paid. Not that Ophelia could afford a lawyer. Another drawback she might have considered before committing the crime. "It's complicated."

"I've had enough of this." The lawyer rolled her eyes and began to march away, toward the rocky incline. She clawed at the boulders in an effort to begin the climb, lodging her feet into any space she could find and scuffing some expensive-looking boots in the process.

And she was wearing jeans. Who wore *jeans* to go canoeing? Ophelia might have been mad, but at least she had the good sense to never wear jeans again on account of how uncomfortable and impractical they were.

Not that her tweed dress was much better.

"You're not dressed as though you're prepared for the outdoors," Ophelia couldn't help but point out, tucking her coat closer to her chest.

"Well, I wasn't quite expecting to experience so *much* of the outdoors today. My apologies." She glared at Ophelia over her shoulder. "And I could say the same of you."

"I suppose I wasn't expecting this either," Ophelia admitted. She staggered closer when the woman's fingers slipped and she grunted in an effort to steady herself. "You're going to hurt yourself. Please, let's just talk first."

"Isn't there another way back?"

"No. Not that I know of. Maybe if we find the road... "

The woman let out a frustrated sigh and, defeated, hopped back onto flat ground, raking her hair out of her face. Her next course of action was to root around in her life jacket, producing a phone a moment later. The screen looked more like a kaleidoscope as she tried to turn it on. "Great. Marvellous. You drowned my phone, too. Do you have yours? We could call for rescue."

In her rush to get out, Ophelia had left her phone at the museum. She shook her head meekly. "Sorry."

The lawyer bit her lip, her eyes falling back to the bubbling river. "Then how am I supposed to get home?"

Sympathy softened Ophelia, though the woman's features remained taut, unreadable. "We can figure that out once we've made a fire, but we can't stay here. We'll freeze." *Or end up kidnapped by criminals*, she thought, but it didn't seem wise to say so.

The woman blinked. "Who even *are* you?"

Ophelia couldn't answer. She didn't know herself these days. She'd always been adventurous and impulsive and so determined that she usually ended up getting into trouble somehow, but she'd never imagined the ring bringing *this* much bad luck. Maybe this was another curse, another unfortunate turn of events brought on by Eilidh and her forsaken relic. The sooner Ophelia got rid of it, the better.

"I'm Ophelia," she said finally. "And you are?"

"Luce," the woman answered coldly, as though Ophelia had forced her to reveal the information against her will.

"Luce. Luce the lawyer," Ophelia remarked. "All right, then. Let's find some shelter, shall we, Luce?"

Luce crossed her arms over her chest and nodded. "Fine. Lead the way."

Ophelia was more than happy to oblige.

* * *

Luce watched through narrowed eyes as the madwoman who had dragged her down a river and into the woods to find a cave aggressively rubbed two sticks together in the shadows. Luce had perched on a boulder to inspect her wounds — which had only begun to sting once the shock had worn off — but, after catching a damp patch of blood on her knee oozing through her jeans, had decided against it, and now flickered between observing Ophelia's unsuccessful attempts at starting a fire and searching for a way out of this madness.

"It's too damp in here. You'll never start a fire," she pointed out finally.

"Won't I?" Ophelia retorted, her elbows jerking harder as she quickened her motions. Eventually, Luce stood corrected. A spark flew from the sticks, faint and easily extinguished, but still there. Ophelia's features brightened, and she let out a confident "Aha!"

Luce only rolled her eyes, tilting her face upward. The mottled gray ceiling was caked in moss and studded with the beginnings of stalactites. The darkness left Luce dizzy, uneasy, as though she were still being tugged along the river current with nothing to clutch on to. Soon night would fall outside, too, and then how would she find her way back?

What if there *was* no way back?

"There we are!" Ophelia exclaimed a few moments later. Luce snapped her focus back to find amber embers glowing with promise. Ophelia blew on them lightly, causing them to spread into flames. They licked along the collection of twigs and pine needles, and Ophelia warmed her palms above them before feeding the fire with more kindling she'd gathered on their short walk here. They weren't too far from the river; Luce could still hear the burbling water below the cawing of jackdaws in the trees shrouding them.

With a sigh, Luce rose and found a dry patch of stone by the fire, wincing when her damp clothes scratched her raw skin like velcro. She still wore her life vest as though it might keep her afloat, but a part of her felt as though she'd already drowned in that river. She was numb and disoriented and floating above her own body. It still didn't stop the frequent pangs of panic from stealing her breath. It was taking every bit of strength in her not to break down and beg Ophelia to take her back to the cabin.

"You're bleeding," Ophelia pointed out, eyeing Luce's beaten appearance with concern. Luce glanced down at her own body, finding that as well as the bloody knee, her once-white jumper was covered in tears and dirt and her hands were scraped and blistered from clutching onto the tree branch so tightly in the river.

"Yes, well, a few scrapes are the least of my problems." The breeze picked up, whistling through the cave and causing the fire to waver. Ophelia chucked more branches onto it, thicker ones now that allowed the flames to grow. The heat warmed Luce's face, and she shuffled closer, closing her eyes against the smoke. "You owe me an explanation."

"I do." Ophelia pursed her lips, her gaze intense with sincerity. The fire reflected in her pupils and turned the blue irises around them to a strange, silvery green. Luce wished she could read what else swam in them. She was usually good at reading people, usually knew within moments whether she would trust her client on a case or find holes in their statements she'd have to patch up. But Ophelia was unreadable and peculiar, and there was something almost ancient hiding behind her smooth features.

Without continuing or offering what was promised, Ophelia slipped her fingers down the cuffed sleeve of her coat and pulled out a white handkerchief with a flourish a moment later.

"Are you an amateur magician as well as a woman on the run, now?" Luce asked, raising a brow.

Ophelia's lips quivered with a repressed smirk as she extended the handkerchief over the fire. "No. For your hands."

"Oh." Luce took it, scrubbing the dirt away from her wounds until the embroidered flowers patterning the cloth were sullied.

A growling distracted her. Luce lifted her head with dread, half expecting a bear to pop out and try to ravage them both, or maybe a wolf. She wasn't sure what creatures lived in Scottish woods or caves. In fact, she'd made it a habit to never try to find out, and it had been going well for the first twenty-nine years of her life.

"Sorry." Ophelia bowed her head with a sheepish smile. "I only had a small lunch."

Luce relaxed with relief and scrambled through the inside pockets of her coat. She came first to her waterlogged phone, and then her emergency beta-blockers, tampons, and a cereal bar, all of which were now soggy. Still, it was all she had, so she offered out the cereal bar to Ophelia and then tucked the anxiety medication away on her tongue, swallowing down the small pink pill without caring if Ophelia saw. She regretted not bringing her antidepressants now, too, though she'd never have expected to need them for what was only supposed to be a couple of hours canoeing. She'd be due her next dose tomorrow morning, and they were just another reason she needed to get back as soon as possible.

"Oh, thank you!" Ophelia smiled and ripped into the cereal bar without a moment's hesitation, breaking it in half. "Want some?"

Luce's stomach twisted at the thought of eating, and she shook her head. "No, thanks. You have it."

"I'll save you some for later." After wrapping the leftover half back into its foil, Ophelia chowed down and then swiped her hands together to get rid of the crumbs.

"Why were those men chasing you?" Luce tucked her knees into the soft pillow of her life vest, feeling her bones slowly unlock against the warmth of the fire.

"They want something that I have."

"What?"

"A ring," Ophelia admitted, pulling something out of her pocket and showing it to Luce. A silver band sat in the palm of her cold-reddened, bruised hand, a blue stone embedded in its center. It wasn't unlike the ring Luce had been gifted from her mother on her birthday last year, with her sapphire birthstone, the one currently on the fourth finger of her right hand.

"A ring," Luce repeated, disbelief numbing her at first, and then, as the words sank in. "A fucking *ring*? I'm here because of *that*?"

"It's complicated." Ophelia frowned and snatched the ring away. "They're con men and they want the stone. It's Hebridean sapphire: very rare and expensive, apparently."

Luce scoffed. "So bloody well let them have it!"

"I can't." Ophelia's voice remained calm, rational, and Luce hated her for it. At least if Ophelia were as panicked or angry or defensive as she was, Luce could have understood something. Anything. As it was, nothing made sense. *Ophelia* didn't make sense. She had embroidered handkerchiefs up her bloody sleeves and dressed like a sweet, trendy old grandmother but was on the run from con men like some sort of character in a

Tom Cruise film.

"Why not?"

"Because… I found the ring up in the mountains. It's part of a local legend, and so I brought it back to Farnoch three years ago and had it exhibited in the museum. Its history matters more than its value, and… well, I need to get it back to where it belongs."

Luce's face scrunched with bewilderment. "You're taking it back after having it displayed in a museum?"

"Yes."

"Won't the museum have something to say about that?"

Ophelia shrugged and nibbled on her chapped bottom lip wearily. Her hair was drying in soft curls at the nape of the neck, slipping free of the bun it had been tied in earlier. She was unlike anybody Luce had ever come across before, and she could do nothing but stare, wait, try to understand even when her own world was crumbling around her.

"I can't explain it without sounding as though I've gone absolutely bonkers," she said finally.

"We passed absolutely bonkers three waterfalls ago," Luce replied.

A soft laugh of agreement fell from Ophelia, and she fiddled with the buttons on her coat. "All right. Fine. The truth is… I'm cursed. The ring is cursed, and so am I for taking it from the lake I found it in. I have to bring it back to lift the curse, and I can't do that if the men who want the sapphire take it from me."

"Cursed," Luce echoed, pursing her lips into a thin line. "You're right. You have gone absolutely bonkers."

Ophelia's eyes snapped to Luce, and the desperation in them made them piercing. Piercing enough that Luce couldn't find it in her to mock her again. Bonkers or not, Ophelia truly believed what she was saying.

Luce would have to humor her. "What makes you think the ring is cursed?"

"The old legend behind it says so. The ring was made by a blacksmith named Tavish after he found the sapphire in the lake near his village over a hundred years ago. He gave it to his wife, Eilidh, as a wedding gift, but not weeks after, Eilidh found him in their bed with another woman. She found out that Tavish had been cheating on her for months, and the ring was more a sign of his guilt than of the strength of their marriage." Ophelia sucked in a ragged breath. "As the story goes, Eilidh told Tavish that he was forgiven. She didn't want the village to know that their marriage was in shambles, and she had two children to think of. Tavish promised Eilidh that he wouldn't see his lover again, that he would be faithful — but he didn't keep to his word, and soon enough rumors began to circulate. When Eilidh caught him cheating a second time, she snapped. She asked him to meet her by the lake not far from their village — the lake where they met — and there, after confronting him in a fit of rage, she tried to drown him. The only problem was that Tavish dragged her into the water, too, and they both died in their struggle to be free of one another.

"When their bodies were recovered and Eilidh's daughter, Cora, was of age, the ring was passed on to her. But it wasn't long before the curse found her, too, and her lover died while at war. Of course, nobody believed in the curse then; it was likely to be a coincidence. But after Cora married another man and had children with him, her husband abandoned her for a younger woman, and they ran away together.

"After that, Cora began to grow suspicious of the ring,

especially as she learned the truth behind her parents' story. In her heartache, she wanted nothing more to do with it. She kept it locked away. Even after, though, there were other tales. Descendants who wore the ring often died spinsters or widowers or jilted divorcées. Somehow, in the end, it ended up back in the lake — probably thrown in by somebody who'd had enough of its curse. *I* was the fool who disturbed it, and now... well, now I have the curse."

Luce might have laughed had the tale not been so intricately woven. As it was, she could only blink and ask, "And what makes you think that you're cursed, other than the utter load of rubbish you've just spewed out?"

Ophelia's lips parted as though she was offended. "Did you listen to anything I just said?"

"Unfortunately, yes. I listened to the part where you dragged me down a river and almost had me drowned because some woman had a slimy cheat of a husband — which, by the way, isn't anything new — a hundred years ago. People cheat and die. Relationships end. Blaming it on a curse won't change that."

"Maybe you're right. Maybe it's all just coincidence and the curse is just something to blame. But I *need* something to blame." Ophelia's chin wobbled with the promise of tears, and a faint wave of guilt swallowed Luce. She hadn't meant to be cruel — she was just irritated and cold and lost, and she still hadn't been offered a valid reason as to why.

Ophelia pulled out the ring again, studying it with glassy eyes. "I don't know if the curse is real, but it feels real to me, and I have to make sure. I have to do anything I can to stop it. I'm sorry that I've dragged you into this, but... I have to take it back to the lake."

"You have to take me back to my cabin!" Luce retorted, scraping her knotted hair back in frustration.

"I don't know if I can. It's going dark now, and Leonard will probably still be looking for me. I need to get to the lake before they do."

A headache was beginning to throb behind Luce's temples, and she pinched the bridge of her nose, simmering with frustration. "So you're just going to leave me here, lost?"

"You could come with me," Ophelia offered.

An acidic, humorless laugh fell from Luce at the very idea. She would rather be locked in that cabin all week than hike her way up a mountain to help a stranger lift a nonexistent curse. "No. No, you got me here, and you'll take me back. *Now*."

"I can't. I told you—"

Panic clogged Luce's throat, her control, her solid ground, slipping between her fingers for one of too many times today. "I can't just stay here!"

Ophelia softened sympathetically, shuffling around the fire so that they were closer — almost knee to knee. "I'm desperate, Luce. Really desperate."

So am I, Luce wanted to say, but she couldn't unseal her mouth. It felt as though her tongue was stuck in thick tar, and it was trickling down her throat, into her windpipe, hardening her lungs and turning her to stone.

"Maybe I could take you first thing in the morning. It might be safer then."

Luce wasn't sure she could survive a night like this, but if she let herself be carried away by the maelstrom of panic and fear and dread whirling in her, she wasn't sure she'd ever find a way out. What else could she do? She didn't know how to get back to the lodge alone, and she had no way of calling for help. She didn't trust or agree with Ophelia and her motivations, but the woman at least had some handy survival skills, and that would keep her alive for tonight.

Exhausted and refusing to beg again, Luce only shook her head and pulled her coat tighter around her body to preserve warmth. "First thing," she repeated frostily. It was the last word she said to Ophelia for the rest of the night.

Chapter Five

L uce rose from the cave floor on stiff, frozen limbs when dawn broke through the trees. She hadn't slept a wink, her night spent jumping at the slightest of sounds — an owl hooting, a twig snapping, water dripping — and watching the fire die to nothing but orange embers.

Ophelia hadn't slept, either. They'd caught eyes over the smoke a few times, and Luce hated that the stranger was her only comfort in the unfamiliar shadows. Not that they'd spoken. Apparently, Luce had hit a nerve last night, and she had no desire to apologize for her quite understandable reaction to Ophelia's story of cursed rings and marital murder.

"Where are you going?" Ophelia asked as Luce dusted the dead leaves and pine needles from her clothes, stretching her limbs to get her blood flowing again.

She felt like a stranger in her own body, even more so than usual. She was dirty and cold and damp and numb, and some part of her had shut down rather than confront reality — an instinct of self-preservation that usually only kicked in before big court cases or the worst days of her anxiety, when she could only just manage to have a shower without suffering from a panic attack.

The problem now, of course, was that she needed the bathroom. The stress of the night had played havoc with her guts, not to mention the half cereal bar she'd nibbled at upon waking. The sooner she returned to civilization, the better.

"Where do you *think* I'm going?" Luce returned finally. "Back to the lodge. Back to bloody normality. As far away from you as I can bloody get."

Ophelia rolled her eyes. "Are you always this hostile?"

"No." Forcing a saccharine smile, Luce finally locked eyes with Ophelia. "It's reserved for people who get me lost in the arse-end of nowhere."

"I told you I'd get you back, but if you'd rather go alone…"

"Frankly," Luce snapped, marching out of the cave, "I couldn't care less anymore. I'm leaving whether you want to come or not."

"You're going the wrong way," Ophelia called, and without turning, Luce could hear the smirk in her voice.

She scoffed and whipped on her heel, the motion causing the hard insoles of her boots to chafe against her damp, socked feet. She would be covered in blisters by the time she got back. She'd come prepared for a spa break rather than an outdoors trip that would end in hikes and capsized canoes, and had dressed accordingly.

Ophelia followed, always three steps behind, as Luce trod through a break in the rocks into the sunrise-dappled forest. She couldn't pretend as though she wasn't glad for Ophelia's lingering presence, if only because she'd already be lost by now without her. The morning was crisp and laced by a layer of frost, the fresh promise of spring lingering with the low, broken clouds and pink patches of sky above them. It was a miracle she hadn't caught hypothermia already.

After what felt like hours — and very well could have been, for Luce had lost all sense of time — of stumbling through the woods without a clear path, weaving through trees while avoiding both stinging nettles and the unidentified crap of various wild animals, the trees began to thin. A wash of gray, watery light tugged Luce forward where it had only been sheer desperation before. Finally, they fell out into a field that yawned out for miles. A farmhouse nestled between the rising hills before them, tiny from such a distance and spewing out smoke from its chimney.

"Oh, thank God." Luce trapped a hysterical laugh behind her hand, relief sifting through her. She was in the real world again, one step closer to shelter. She would never take her bed or shower or a good cup of tea for granted again.

"We should see if someone might give you a lift back to Alasdair Ridge," Ophelia suggested. "It can't be too far away now. An hour or two at most."

"That's the best idea you've had since we met." Luce winced as she set off again up the first incline, blisters beginning to form on her heels. Gritting her teeth, she buried her boots into the soft soil and forced herself to keep going. Her knotted stomach growled with both anticipation and hunger, her bladder and bowels ready to burst. She wouldn't have made it much further had they not found the farmhouse.

A fat raindrop splashed onto Luce's nose. She didn't care if it rained anymore, too focused on the farmhouse.

"Luce!" Ophelia called after a few minutes more.

Breathless and desperate, Luce ignored her.

Chapter Five

"*Luce!*" Ophelia repeated, louder now — and further away.

With a huff, Luce turned around to find Ophelia pointing in the direction of the woods. Luce followed her gesture — and froze. Not a few meters away, a herd of cattle watched Luce with eerily fixed gazes. They weren't the adorable black-and-white cows Luce was used to seeing on the sides of motorways, either. These ones were horned, with brown, shaggy coats: Highland cattle.

"Don't move!" Ophelia warned. "They're not usually aggressive, but they have calves with them."

Luce had already noticed the small calves at their mother's sides. She knew from all sorts of documentaries and news articles that cows were protective of their calves — sometimes to the point of aggression.

She might well be fucked.

"What should I do?" Luce lifted her hands in front of her slowly, as though the cows were police officers and she was a cornered criminal submitting to arrest.

"Stay there."

Luce had no intention of moving until the cow at the front took a step forward. Instinct pushed her stumbling back to keep the distance. The cow grunted and Luce could have sworn she saw its eyes flash with threat.

It took another step forward, and Luce ran.

"Luce!" Ophelia's shouts grew fainter as Luce tore away, her ankles snapping against the uneven slope of earth.

She glanced over her shoulder and wished she hadn't. The herd of cattle were chasing her, tearing up the dirt with their heavy hooves. Ophelia trailed behind them hopelessly.

"Why aren't they chasing *you*?" Luce screamed, her shins beginning to splinter. "You're the one with the cursed ring!"

"Maybe they just sense one of their own!" Ophelia responded.

Luce might have come up with a witty retort had she not been so preoccupied. As it was, she hopped over a rough cluster of rocks, swiftly approaching a barbed-wire fence. She let out a curse and glanced around desperately. There was nowhere to go but uphill or through a small, broken gap in the fence. Her lungs seared with the effort it had taken just to get here, so she chose the latter option.

Ducking her head, Luce climbed carefully through the fence and prayed that the cows wouldn't risk getting caught on barbed wire to get to her.

And then the world slipped from under her feet. She slid down a sloppy patch of mud with nothing to grab on to, rain spraying in her eyes and mouth as an earsplitting shriek rent through the open air. It took Luce a moment to realize that it was coming from her, and kept coming as the slipping and sliding continued. She wasn't sure she would ever stop. Her life was just slimy mud and rain and falling, always falling. Then again, it had always felt this way inside: grimy and scary and dreadful, with Luce never sure what would happen next.

All at once, she skidded to a stop at the bottom of the hill, soil caking her face until she could taste its bitterness. It left her hair matted to her cheek and clung to her clothes like a second layer of skin, heavy and earthy and enough to make her nauseous. Luce couldn't even find it in her to stand. She remained sputtering on the ground in an ever-growing puddle, her fingernails thick with the dirt and grass she had clawed at in an attempt to stop.

She could no longer breathe, either, and wondered if it was also clogging her airways.

Ophelia appeared at the top of the hill, her hand over her

mouth as she found Luce. She ran toward her, avoiding the mudslide carefully, where the imprint of Luce's fall was still smeared. The cows had stopped at the fence behind her, of course.

Luce was beginning to feel like if any of them were cursed, it was her.

"Oh my goodness," Ophelia breathed when she came to a stop beside Luce. "Are you all right?"

Luce had to blow out another clot of mud from her mouth before she could talk again, the rain streaking down her face. "Am I *all right?*" she repeated incredulously. "Yes, I'm bloody splendid, can't you tell?"

"I…" Ophelia stuttered on her own words, her lips quivering with a stifled smile. She was enjoying it, Luce realized with rage sparking through her. "I'm sorry. It's just…" Ophelia muffled a choked laugh with her hands.

Luce's upper lip curled with a bitter, disgusted snarl, and she ignored Ophelia's outstretched hand to pull herself up alone. She didn't even have the energy to blame Ophelia — not aloud, anyway. Instead, she curled her grubby hands into fists so tight that her nails dug into her palms and marched back up the hill, toward the farmhouse. A part of her hoped that Ophelia wouldn't bother to follow.

Of course, she wasn't that lucky.

* * *

The middle-aged woman in the farmhouse took one look at them both and slammed the rotting wood door on their faces. Ophelia couldn't blame her, what with the fact that Luce was covered in mud, but the rain was pelting down now and there was no way they could carry on in this state.

Apparently, Luce thought the same, because she rapped on the door with so much force that Ophelia was surprised her knuckles didn't split. "Excuse me! We need help! Please!"

It took at least sixty seconds of Luce's desperate bangs on the door and a dog barking somewhere within the house before it opened again, creaking on old, rusted hinges. Cobwebs draped across the porch ceiling above them, and old, ruined stone walls surrounded the place. Ophelia had searched desperately for a truck or car or even a tractor on the way up and had found none. Other than the cows in the next field over and the woman glaring at them now, the place looked deserted.

"All right, all right. No more of that ruckus!" the woman scolded in a thick Scottish accent, wedging herself in the doorway as though she was expecting them to invite themselves in. "What do you want? There's nothing for you here."

"I need to get back to the lodge at Alasdair Ridge," Luce said. "Is there any chance you could take me?"

A sharp chuff fell from the woman. "How do you propose I do that? Hmm? By piggyback?"

"You don't have a car?" Luce's shoulders fell, still caked in mud as they were. The rain had slashed through a lot of it, though, and it dripped off her and bled into the gravel. A shred of guilt settled in Ophelia's chest. She'd never meant to drag Luce into so much trouble. She'd never meant for any of this. Yesterday, she'd been working in the museum like any other day. Today, she was stuck in the middle of bloody nowhere with a woman who — quite justifiably — hated her guts, still no closer to lifting Eilidh's curse.

She wondered where Leonard would be now. Ahead of her, probably. But he didn't know the precise location of the High

Mór lake. He hadn't spent weeks hiking in the Highlands like she had, searching for fossils. While he might have been a decent archaeologist once, he now spent his time in lecture halls and offices, and that meant Ophelia had the upper hand — or, at least, she would when she got rid of Luce.

"Have you seen one lying about?" the woman groused with unnecessary bitterness.

"No," Luce replied calmly. "But I hoped—"

"You're out of luck, lass. Go and pester someone else."

The door slammed shut again, and Ophelia narrowed her eyes. She could practically feel the anger rippling off Luce as she banged on the door once more.

"I'm not leaving until you help us!" she shouted.

"Luce," Ophelia said gently. She knew when to retreat from a losing battle. Scottish women were stubborn at the best of times, never mind ones who appeared to live alone in a completely secluded set of hills. "We'll find somewhere else."

"No, we won't!"

"She's not going to help us."

Luce crossed her legs awkwardly, still knocking. A patch of skin on her cheek that was clear of mud had turned a beetroot red. "She's going to bloody have to, otherwise I'm going to piss myself, among other things."

Ah. That explained Luce's determination. Ophelia herself had been desperate for a wee for the past hour, but she'd been waiting for a decent place to stop, and her many years of exploring secluded places had trained her bladder well.

The door swung open once more, and Luce didn't give the woman a chance to scold them again. She placed her hands on her hips, her expression stormier than the current torrent raining down on them. "Listen. I need to use your toilet whether you like it or not. I'm covered in mud because I was chased through the fields by blooming *cows*, and I'm stuck in the middle of nowhere when I should be on a spa break getting a facial and eating strawberries. I haven't had anything to eat or drink since yesterday afternoon except half a cereal bar with a dangerous amount of fiber in it this morning because *she*" — Luce jabbed her finger in Ophelia's direction — "hijacked my canoe and sent me down a river. Now, you can either open the door, or I'll be forced to do my business here on your doorstep, because I can no longer hold it in. It's an emergency. *Please*."

The woman pursed her lips and finally stepped aside. "Fine. But hurry up."

Luce had no trouble doing that. She darted into the house and Ophelia was left to shift awkwardly at the doorstep. "I don't suppose I can use it after her?"

The woman rolled her eyes. "Come in."

"Thank you."

Ophelia stepped into the house warily only to be greeted with licks to her hand by a sheepdog with black rings around its eyes. It was about the friendliest anybody had been to her in the last twenty-four hours, and she bent down to stroke behind its ears. "Who do we have here?"

"That's Floss. Don't think you can trust her. She'll tear off your hand if I ask her to."

Ophelia doubted such a gentle dog would do anything so vicious, but she pretended to be convinced, pulling her hand away to stand again. The house was cold and drafty and full of shadows and dust, the furniture lackluster and mismatched. She supposed the woman didn't get many guests. "I'm sorry again about the intrusion, but… I was wondering if you might have a map of the nearby area."

She huffed as though Ophelia had asked her for a kidney, wandering to a crooked bookshelf and tracing her hands along the spines. Ophelia smiled in relief. If she couldn't get warmth and shelter here, she would at least know where to head.

The woman pulled out a large book — an atlas of the Scottish Highlands — and offered it to Ophelia.

"Thank you," Ophelia said, taking it gratefully.

"So what are you two, then? Hikers who took a wrong turn?" She wandered over to the kitchen, whose wonky cupboards seemed to hang on the wall by a single nail, and filled up an old-fashioned kettle before putting it on a gas stove. Ophelia prayed she would be offered a hot drink, but didn't dare get her hopes up, instead following the woman and taking a seat at the kitchen table. Floss followed her and sat at her feet, yawning to show off her canines. *Vicious beast indeed.*

"No. Well, sort of. I'm an archaeologist, but, er... I've run into a bit of trouble," Ophelia murmured, her brows knitting together as she flicked through the pages of the atlas. Finally she found one that pinpointed High Mór. It was a shame she only had a vague idea of where she was now. She could at least point out Alasdair Ridge, but how far they had strayed from it after hurtling down the river and walking miles this morning, she had no clue. "Where exactly are we at the moment?"

"An archaeologist? What are you hoping to find around here?" As the kettle began to whistle, she meandered back over, thrusting her index finger on a spot just west of Farnoch and Alasdair Ridge. Good. They hadn't strayed too far then. "Here."

"Thank you." Ophelia tried to memorize her next route, first to Alasdair Ridge and then north toward High Mór. The journey back to Alasdair Ridge would set her well back, but if she could manage to get hold of supplies and some decent walking shoes, she might be able to speed up her hike to make up for it — unless the weather stayed like this or Leonard found her, that was.

Doubt crept in, and with it a hint of defeat. Her chances of reaching the lake seemed to lessen with every passing second, and she wasn't sure what she'd been thinking in rushing to the trail in the first place. She needed gear, shelter, sustenance, and she'd come charging in wearing a bloody skirt, with no other supplies.

Maybe she should go back to Farnoch after dropping Luce off. Her car was still at the lodge, and she could collect her camping gear back at her cottage — but what if someone caught her? What if they were already looking for her and the ring? What if Morag had called the police?

It wasn't worth the risk. Nothing was. No matter what trouble it brought, Ophelia had to free herself of the curse, and she couldn't do that if she was caught.

She'd forgotten about the woman's question until footsteps sounded from the hallway. She lifted her gaze from the map, finding Luce standing in the hallway only slightly cleaner than she had been before. "I wouldn't recommend going in there for a while."

The woman's narrowed eyes flew back to Ophelia. "You were saying?"

"Right. Yes. I'm actually not hoping to find anything this time around. I'm trying to return an artifact to the place it belongs."

Luce rolled her eyes and sat at the table across from Ophelia. "She thinks it's cursed."

"What's cursed?"

Ophelia sucked in a breath and closed the atlas. "I don't

suppose you've heard of Eilidh's ring."

"Everybody around here has." The woman paused, looking Ophelia up and down curiously. "Don't tell me *you* have it."

"Guilty." For the first time in the last twenty-four hours, Ophelia felt comfortably warm, and she shucked off her coat so that she wouldn't feel the cold as much when they were inevitably turfed out and left to fend for themselves again.

"And the curse?"

"If it's not real, it's awfully coincidental that I've had some terrible luck ever since finding it."

"But surely they wouldn't just let you take the ring back. It must be worth a small fortune. Everybody on Skye knows the tale."

Ophelia nodded her agreement and hoped that the woman lacked a telephone line as well as a car. The last thing she needed was another person to run from if the police were called. "Somebody else attempted to steal it. Con men after the Hebridean sapphire in the band. When I'm not researching, I work at the museum in Farnoch, so I thought it best to put the ring back myself before anybody else could take it."

"I see." The woman moved back to the stove as the kettle shrieked to a boil, turning the gas off and extinguishing the blue ring of flame. "Would the two of you like some tea?"

Ophelia slumped in relief. There was nothing she wanted more — save for the lifting of the curse, at least.

Luce's eyes widened with the same enthusiasm, and she nodded erratically. "I would *sell my soul* for some tea. Please."

As somebody who had accidentally fallen into a similar trap, Ophelia wouldn't have recommended that, but instead of pointing it out, she ran her hands through Floss's soft white fur and let a sprinkle of hope reignite in her belly.

Maybe she would get to High Mór after all.

Chapter Six

～⚬ഉ⚬～

Somehow, Luce and Ophelia had managed to earn a place to stay until the rain stopped. Between the fire crackling in an old-fashioned grate and the hot bath she'd just dissolved into for the past hour, Luce would be quite happy to stay here for the foreseeable future. At least it would give her a chance to recharge, and she certainly felt more human now that she had eaten and washed off the muck.

The woman — Enid, she'd finally introduced herself over their hot cups of tea — had even left them some fresh clothes to change into. The fleecy jumper and waterproof trousers weren't Luce's usual style and they held the faint smell of dust and potpourri, but her own clothes were in the washing machine, probably ruined, so they'd do for now. She slipped them on quickly in the bedroom, trying not to glance at the doorway to the bathroom, where Ophelia was bathing. It didn't have a lock on it — she supposed somebody who lived alone in the middle of the hills didn't need locks — and she could just make out the knots of Ophelia's spine, the pale skin stretched over them, her damp, rusty-brown hair tangled at the nape of her neck.

Heat crept up Luce's neck, and she looked away quickly. It must have been Stockholm syndrome. Ophelia had practically kidnapped her, and now Luce was trying not to look at her naked body. Stockholm syndrome. There was no other explanation.

When Ophelia began to rise out of the bath, the water trickling down her body, Luce distracted herself by sitting down with the thermal socks Enid had left out for her, unrolling them so that she could slip them on before her feet got cold again. Red blisters had swelled across her heels and toes, and she winced.

"Ouch."

Luce lifted her gaze and found Ophelia hovering above her, wrapped in a towel that only covered her from the large crest of her bust to her curvy, dimpled thighs. The fact did not help Luce's blush, and she prayed it wasn't as noticeable as it felt as she poked at her blisters.

"Don't do that!" Ophelia warned, tightening the knot at her cleavage. "Let me see if Enid has any plasters."

She wandered off, her bare feet leaving wet prints on the old wooden floor, and then returned a moment later waving a box of plasters proudly. Luce smiled gratefully, expecting Ophelia to give them to her —

But Ophelia didn't. Instead, she crouched in front of Luce with a hand still wrapped cautiously around her towel, pulling out the first plaster and peeling it from its packaging. Luce frowned and removed her hand from the biggest blister, and it seemed instinct for Ophelia to stick it on the angry, red lesion with gentle, steady fingers. Drops of water snaked around her neck from the tips of her hair, curling down her pale skin, across her collarbone and silver stretch marks, into her towel, and Luce could do nothing but watch, stunned to silence, frozen lest a sudden movement scared Ophelia away.

But Ophelia stayed to bandage the second blister, and then the third, as Luce tried to distract herself from the blazing heat prickling through her.

"Swap," said Ophelia with a gentle pat.

Luce did, balancing her other foot on Ophelia's bare thigh so that she could get better access. Her rough sole grazed soft, dewy skin, and somehow, it was the most intimate position Luce had ever found herself in. Ophelia didn't even seem to notice. Her teeth sank into her plump bottom lip in concentration, and Luce couldn't breathe. She was used to not being able to breathe, of course, but this was different. This sucked the air from her lungs and replaced it with tender warmth rather than brittle ice, and she wasn't sure what was passing between them or when she had started reacting to Ophelia so familiarly. She was only sure that she liked it.

Definitely Stockholm syndrome.

It was Floss who saved Luce from having to think about it for much longer. She bounded in with what appeared to be a sheep plush toy in her mouth, her tail wagging joyfully. Luce shifted away and put her feet back on the floor. She was wary around animals, just as she was with everything else. Ophelia, on the other hand, laughed and fussed over the sheepdog as though she were her own.

"Dinner's ready!" Enid's voice floated in behind Floss.

"I'll, er, let you get dressed." Luce slipped on her socks and left the room, Floss trailing behind her. She was glad to be free of the strange tension building in the bedroom, though she still thought of the towel brushing Ophelia's pale skin, the ghost of her touch still dancing across Luce's feet.

The rich aroma of fresh peppers and tomatoes greeted her when she reached the kitchen, and her stomach growled embarrassingly loudly, putting an end to any ideas of romance.

"Hungry?" Enid smirked.

Luce's mouth watered as she replied, "Starving."

* * *

Ophelia devoured the soup and buttered slices of crusty bread as though she had been starved for years rather than just a day. Outside, the rain had ebbed to a light patter against the windows, and Ophelia almost lamented the fact that she would have to leave soon. It was cozy in the farmhouse, with Floss always keeping her ankles warm and the smell of homemade food reminding her of long, snug winters buried in handkerchiefs from the sniffles.

And there was Luce. Luce still had to get back to the lodge. Ophelia no longer knew how she would get the ring back to the lake before Leonard and Hector found her.

"Have you always lived here alone?" Luce asked, swiping her bread around her bowl to soak up the last dregs of soup.

Enid's lips curved into a wistful grin, her eyes glistening absently. "No, not always."

Ophelia frowned. "It must get lonely out here, all on your own. Well, except for Floss, of course," she added, petting Floss's head under the table to show she hadn't forgotten about her.

Enid only shrugged. "Sometimes. Then again, people are arseholes and… well. I lost the only one I could tolerate."

Only then did Ophelia notice the golden band gleaming

on the fourth finger of Enid's left hand, not unlike the one on her own. Sympathy sank in her stomach. Sympathy and understanding. "You were married."

"I was."

"What happened?"

"The bastard made me a widower." It was said in jest, but sadness laced Enid's tone. She collected their bowls and placed them in the sink distractedly.

The sight left Ophelia smothered in a grief she'd thought she'd left behind, a grief that had faded and remolded itself to fit around her ever since her first loss, a grief that usually only came out at night now, when it was dark and she lay alone on his side of the bed, where it could wrap its arms around her the way he used to do.

It was what left her admitting rawly, "I'm sorry. I… I know how it feels to lose someone you love. I lost my fiancé, too."

Surprise flashed across Luce's features, a line sinking in the space between her brows. "When?"

Ophelia cleared her throat of its lump. It still hurt to talk about. She had a feeling it always would. "Three years ago."

"Ophelia—"

"It's hard work, loving someone. Even harder losing them," Enid cut in, scrubbing the plates with renewed vigor. Her head was bowed, her features pinched in the faint reflection of the window, settled in front of a row of tall evergreen trees and pale green-and-yellow hills. "I came here after he died because… well, because he was the love of my life. There'll never be another him, and I didn't want to live the same life with neighbors I bloody well hated without him there, pretending it's okay. We always dreamt of buying a wee place like this and doing it up. So I did it. Here, I'm alone. I can talk to him whenever I want, and nobody bothers me. Nobody expects anything from me."

Ophelia thought she understood somehow, though she'd left that mindset behind long ago. Losing Peter had been awful and it had taken her a while to get used to life without him — but it had been his end, not hers. More than the grief and the missing him, she blamed herself for coming across Eilidh's ring. She'd killed him. And she'd only realized as much, believed as much, once she'd tried to start dating again over a year later and found her attempts completely unsuccessful.

But she was here because she was ready to love again. She was trying to lift the curse because her heart was too big to not share it with somebody else. Maybe she didn't deserve to move on. Maybe Peter would have hated her for trying. But she had to find a way. If she was sure of anything, she was sure that people could fall in love more than just once. And Ophelia wanted more than anything to at least have the chance, without devastation knocking at her door because she carried a century-old curse with her.

"I sometimes wish I could be like that," Luce admitted, bowing her head and focusing on a splotch of spilled soup on the table. "I can't turn my brain off. Even if I lived here, alone, I wouldn't be happy. If nobody else expects anything of me, I still always expect too much of myself, and if I stop for even a moment..." She trailed off as though realizing that she was sharing a part of her she didn't want to.

Ophelia wished she could hear the end of that sentence, but she didn't dare pry. Not with Luce. Not after everything they'd endured in the last twenty-four hours. Instead, sympathy softened her as they locked eyes.

"What about you?" Enid's attention turned back to Ophelia.

She leaned against the kitchen sink, her shirt damp and sud-covered from washing up. "You say you're cursed by Eilidh's ring? Has it something to do with your fiancé?"

"Every woman who's ever owned the ring has ended up widowed or divorced or alone," Ophelia murmured, dragging the sleeves of the oversized knitted jumper that Enid had loaned her over her hands. "I check two out of three of those boxes. Peter died not long after I found the ring, and recent attempts at moving on have proved futile. My love life" — she let out a humorless laugh, thick with oncoming tears — "is in shambles. Bloody Eilidh, eh?"

Enid narrowed her eyes. "Maybe you just haven't found the right person to move on with."

"Maybe. But... I can't take the risk. This curse feels too real, and I want it gone. I have to."

Luce remained suspiciously silent, picking at her nails and not meeting either of their eyes. Ophelia found herself wishing she understood Luce more: how her brain worked; why she was so closed off, so difficult to talk to. It felt like more than just the fact that Ophelia had dragged her into trouble. It felt like something to do with what she'd just said, about not being able to stop or lower her expectations.

"Well, I suppose now you're both here, you're welcome to stay until the rain stops," offered Enid. "I have an old camping bed I can sleep on if you two want to take the double."

Ophelia grimaced. The last thing she wanted to do was intrude upon Enid's clear love for privacy and put herself back another night. But even if she set off now, she'd have to take Luce back first. She'd promised. Besides, soon it would be going dark, and she wasn't sure if she'd be able to make a journey up into the mountains without being able to see where she was going.

"I don't know if that's a good idea."

"You won't get to High Mór this evening, dear. At least if you set off tomorrow well rested and on a full belly, you can make a decent go of it."

That was true. Ophelia hadn't slept last night, and she still felt drained because of it. Whether she set off now or tomorrow morning, she was bound to be behind Leonard. This would be the only offer of shelter and a decent night's rest for the next couple of days.

But Luce surely wouldn't want to stay a minute longer. She'd been so desperate to get back.

Ophelia looked at her in question, and Luce shrugged. "I'm exhausted, and it's still bouncing down outside. I'd much rather stay here, to be honest. It's nice, not being drenched and covered in shite. Do you happen to have a phone, by the way? I could call a cab back to the lodge tomorrow."

Enid scoffed. "You'll have a hard time getting a cab around here, lass. No, I don't have a phone. They melt your brain, those things."

Ophelia wasn't surprised, since the woman also lacked a television or any other piece of technology from the twenty-first century. She couldn't blame her, though. It must be a simpler, easier life. One of the reasons Ophelia had always enjoyed history was the utter difference in lifestyle for people of the past. She had done all her studying in dusty old libraries, her nose always stuck in books rather than glued to a computer screen. She admired Enid, if anything — even if she also sympathized with her loss.

"Either way, I'm staying the night. Thank you, Enid. If you want to be on your way, Ophelia, you can."

Ophelia itched to do just that — but she knew as well as Luce and Enid did that she wouldn't get very far. So, reluctantly, Ophelia sighed and lazed back in her chair. "All right. I suppose it would be better to set off on a decent night's sleep. I don't suppose you have any pudding, Enid?"

"Funnily enough" — Enid grinned, pulling a towel-covered dish from the fridge — "I do."

She lifted the tea towel to reveal a perfectly golden, thick-crusted apple crumble, untouched and dusted with sugar. The smell of cinnamon, of autumn, wafted around the kitchen, and Ophelia couldn't help but grin and lick her lips hungrily. "I like you, Enid."

"Well. I suppose you two aren't so bad yourself, for people."

The compliment was good enough for Ophelia.

Chapter Seven

L uce crawled into bed at seven p.m. without caring that it was too early. In the kitchen, Ophelia was still devouring Enid's apple crumble while they chatted, and though Luce knew she might seem rude to miss out on it, she was too tired, too desperate for some quiet, to stick around. She needed some alone time, some space to calm her anxiety. She needed time to breathe and recover. She needed time to prepare for another day tomorrow.

The sudden silence brought her back to her body, and she swallowed deep breaths as her eyes adjusted to the low light of the bedside lamp. The bedsheets were scratchy and smelled of Floss's dusty fur, but anything was better than sleeping in a cave. She'd sidled as close to the edge of the mattress as possible for when Ophelia joined her, tucked in the fetal position. Her arms were still locked with a tension that she couldn't let go of.

Her brain seemed to flutter in her skull when she closed her eyes, like a faint bolt of lightning lancing through the constant fog in her head. It was a familiar feeling, and one that left her stomach twisting with more dread. It was her body's way of reminding her that she hadn't taken her antidepressants for at least thirty-six hours. Not since she'd left her house in Manchester in the early hours of yesterday morning.

She tried to put it out of her mind. Worrying about it wouldn't help, and there was nothing she could do about it until tomorrow. She could manage until then. She would have to.

Still, her nerves hummed, a constant drone that never gave her any peace, and she tossed and turned to try to get more comfortable, more relaxed.

It didn't work.

Ophelia wandered in about an hour later, padding quietly in an attempt to not disturb Luce. Luce kept her eyes closed, her fingers clenched in the duvet as Ophelia's weight pressed onto the springy mattress and she slipped in beside her. Them sharing a bed together was about the least strange thing to have happened in the past day, but still, Ophelia's presence against Luce's back was foreign, and she felt uneasy. Warm from the company, but uneasy. Especially after discovering the truth about Ophelia and her loss. Luce had been so cruel about the curse; she hadn't known, hadn't even suspected. She hadn't even noticed the ring. Ophelia didn't seem plagued by grief the way Enid did. She was so full of energy, so light and unflinching against whatever was thrown at her.

Not like Luce.

Luce rolled onto her back finally, interlocking her fingers across her stomach and sighing. "Are you asleep?"

"No. Are you?"

Luce repressed a laugh, instead shaking her head. "Nope."

Ophelia gave no reply, though Luce could hear her steady

breaths, in and out, rising and falling in equal measure like a gentle tide reaching the shore. Luce wondered what it must be like to be so steady. Her breaths were always shallow against her too-tight lungs: a tempest of crashing waves, always drowning her.

"I just... I wanted to apologize. I didn't know about your fiancé. I can't imagine how it must have felt to lose someone you loved, and I suppose it makes the curse thing a little bit clearer."

"You couldn't have known," Ophelia replied gently. "And you have every right to be angry with me, Luce. I've torn you from your peaceful holiday and gotten you into all sorts of bother. Honestly, I don't even know what I was thinking, running up into the mountains like that without even a sleeping bag to my name. I'm just... I'm desperate."

Luce didn't understand, not really. Curses weren't real. *Her* biggest threat wasn't something external and intangible, but rather her own flesh and blood, her own mind, all of which failed her every day. Still, she could only imagine how Ophelia must have felt after losing her fiancé, and what that sort of grief must have done to her. Luce couldn't keep blaming her for it, even if Ophelia had dragged her into the chaos.

"How did he die?" Luce couldn't help but ask. She whispered it into the dark, as though saying it quietly meant that she might be able to take it back if she needed to.

"Cycling to work, of all things." Ophelia's scoff dripped with bitterness. "He and I spent so much time hiking and traveling and taking risks, and in the end it was just... a cycling accident. It doesn't seem right. He deserved a better death than that."

"I'm sorry." Luce turned over toward Ophelia, her brows knitting together and sympathy clenching in her gut. "But you must know it isn't your fault. Things happen. You taking a ring from a lake couldn't have caused his accident."

Ophelia's eyes found Luce's. They were glossy in the shadows, her eyelashes casting shadows across her cheekbones. "What if it did?"

Luce shook her head. She didn't have the answer that Ophelia wanted. In the end, she was searching for something that could never be proven with empirical evidence, and Luce, of all people, knew how futile such a thing was. You couldn't base an argument on a theory alone.

So instead of trying, she found Ophelia's hand, resting between them at the side of Ophelia's hip, and squeezed.

"Do you still want me to take you home tomorrow?" Ophelia asked, looking down at their intertwined hands. Luce couldn't remember the last time she'd been this close to another person. She couldn't remember the last time she'd wanted to be. Where it had been strange before, it now felt like the most natural, easy thing in her world — and things very rarely felt easy for Luce. She held on, her eyes fluttering when Ophelia's thumb began to trace circles into her knuckle.

The answer should have been yes, and it should have been immediate... and yet Luce couldn't find the resolve, the desperation, she'd felt not an hour ago. Not when she was here, blanketed in Ophelia's warmth, and in the smell of the musky, unlabeled shampoo Enid had let them use, with the essence of savory soup still faint in the air. She focused on these things so that she wouldn't have to notice her heart trying to slam its way out of her ribcage.

But she had to get home. She needed her medication and she needed familiarity and she needed clean clothes, her car, a replacement phone for the waterlogged one left in a pocket somewhere. She needed something to cling to that wasn't Ophelia: normality, mostly. "I should get back… but I don't want to delay you. You need to get to the lake."

Ophelia loosed a ragged sigh and turned so that they were facing one another. Her hair fanned across her face in strands, her soft apple cheeks flattened by the pillow, and Luce could admit to herself for the first time that she was beautiful, with her round, soft features and her doe eyes and the slight overbite that always left her teeth visible when her lips were even a little bit parted.

"I wish you could come," Ophelia admitted quietly. "I know you've hated all of this, but… when you're not completely furious with me, I quite like having you here. Maybe it could be fun, hiking together. And the lake… it's beautiful, Luce. Everything's so peaceful in the mountains. Maybe it would surprise you. Maybe it could help with what you talked about before."

Luce clenched her jaw. She didn't do spontaneous hikes with strangers. She couldn't. But how could she explain that without hurting Ophelia's feelings? How could she explain that she wished she could be different, more relaxed, easier to like, but her anxiety always kept her separated from the world with a jagged sheet of unbreakable glass?

Because when she hadn't been stuck in her own brain, when she'd been walking and sucking in earthy puffs of air and learning about Ophelia at the dinner table, maybe she hadn't hated it so much. When she was running from cows and flying down rivers and trying not to trip over her own feet, maybe she didn't have time to feel the tension, the nerves, she usually felt. Maybe if she hadn't needed her medication, or maybe if she wasn't ill at all, she might have just said yes and gone on an adventure with Ophelia, and maybe she would have liked it. She'd been that sort of person once. She missed being her now.

"I don't know," Luce answered finally. She unclasped their hands and turned her back to Ophelia, tears pricking her eyes. Because she didn't know. And whether she was here or home or in the cabin or halfway up the mountains, she'd never really know what was best for her or what her body needed from her. She'd always just be stuck with a racing heart and an aching stomach and a thick haze of unhappiness, loneliness, fear, in her brain.

"It was a silly idea." Ophelia shifted away from Luce, and it left her cold. "Of course you wouldn't want that. I just... somehow, I keep forgetting that we're strangers."

So did Luce, and perhaps that was part of the problem. Because if Ophelia asked her to come with her again, Luce might be tempted to say yes.

Luce lay awake for a long time, waiting — but Ophelia didn't ask again.

Chapter Eight

Ophelia slipped out of bed as soon as the first rays of sun crept through the curtains. Enid was already up, watching Floss chasing magpies in the fields outside.

"Morning, Enid," Ophelia greeted politely, glancing out of the window herself to assess the weather. The sky was pale and swathed in a buttery haze as it stirred from sleep with the sun, the clouds thin and wispy. It looked promising.

"Morning, dear. How did you sleep?"

"Good," she lied. In truth, it felt as though she'd slept on a rocking boat in the middle of a storm. Luce had tossed and turned and fidgeted and sighed, and even when she'd been still, she'd ground her teeth so loudly that Ophelia was surprised she had any left at all. She was beginning to suspect that Luce was more than just the uptight, angry woman Ophelia had taken her for when they'd met. Perhaps Ophelia was reading too much into it — but after Luce's words at the dinner table yesterday, it felt like something much more. "I was wondering if I could borrow some supplies from you for the hike up to High Mór.

A tent and a sleeping bag, maybe?"

Enid smiled and tapped her nose before heading to the fridge. She pulled out a large Tupperware container. "I've already packed you some sandwiches and dug out my best hiking boots. Size six, aye?"

"Aye…" Ophelia mumbled, taken aback. Yesterday Enid had been slamming a door in her face, and today she was making up packed lunches and going out of her way to help. "Thank you, Enid. Really. You've been so generous."

Enid batted her hand away. "It's been years since I've had company. It's the least I can do for you and the fiancé you lost. Here's hoping Eilidh lifts that bastard curse on you and you turn out a little bit less bitter than me."

"I'll come back when I can and update you on it all." Touched, Ophelia squeezed Enid's shoulder gently. "I'll gather my things together and then we'll be out of your hair."

She did just that, grateful when Enid found her old camping supplies in the shed. They smelled of mildew but were better than nothing, and Ophelia packed them up, wondering if it was time to wake Luce. She hadn't wanted to earlier; she'd looked so peaceful dappled by the dawn, her mouth slightly agape and her dark lashes shuttered. With how restless she'd been all night, it hadn't felt right to disturb her.

"You never did tell me how that Luce of yours ended up here, too." Enid's eyes were curious as she filled Ophelia's flask with hot tea.

"Well… that wasn't planned."

"I thought you two were quite different. A nice girl, though. Misunderstood, I reckon."

Ophelia thought so, too, but that didn't account for the heat suddenly warming her cheeks. She kept her head bowed, hoping Enid wouldn't notice as she hummed her agreement.

"She's worth being patient with, I think." Enid's mouth tugged with a suggestive smirk, and Ophelia frowned. Luce made Ophelia nervous sometimes, yes... but did Enid suspect there was something more between them?

"I don't think she wants my patience, Enid. I think she wants to get as far away from me and all this as possible, and I don't blame her."

"I think some people can surprise you with what they want, dear. Not many, mind, but some. My Owen did, God rest his soul. The two of you reminded me of how we used to be last night, in the early days. You're like chalk and cheese, but the best pairings usually are."

Ophelia wrinkled her nose and sipped her tea. "I don't know about that."

"Don't know about what?" Luce stumbled out of the bedroom, bleary-eyed and disheveled, causing Ophelia to start. Had she heard? But Luce only yawned, stumbling onto one of the kitchen chairs.

"Good morning, sunshine." Ophelia beamed sweetly. "She wakes at last."

"Ugh. No smiling before eight a.m."

"Sleep well?" asked Enid, filling a teacup and placing it in front of Luce.

Luce only shrugged, her features wavering for a moment. Ophelia couldn't help but raise an eyebrow, wondering whether the question she had proposed in the darkness last night had anything to do with Luce's terrible sleep. Ophelia had been silly to expect Luce to come with her, and even sillier to ask her to. She just... wasn't sure she was ready to say goodbye just yet. Though their short time together had been turbulent, Ophelia was finding herself enjoying Luce's company, and if she were honest with herself, she was afraid of bumping into Leonard again all alone. Maybe Enid was right. Maybe they did make a decent pairing, different as they were.

"Well, I'm all packed and ready to go when you are."

"In that case" — Luce clinked her teacup back onto its saucer quickly — "let's go. Thank you for the lovely hospitality, Enid, but I miss Wi-Fi too much to stick around."

"Who's Wi-Fi?" Enid asked with a frown.

Ophelia laughed and slung Enid's backpack onto her shoulder, raring to go herself. She patted down the pocket of her coat to make sure the ring was still there and bade Floss a goodbye with a gentle pat on her head. Before they could set out, though, a knock sounded on the door.

Enid frowned. "Two lots of visitors in less than a day. I'm going to have to bloody well move, aren't I? Do you think I'll be pestered less in Sweden?"

"How often do you usually get visitors?" Ophelia asked, lowering her voice as dread trickled like ice into her belly.

"Never, thank heavens." Enid was already making her way to the door, stepping over a barking Floss.

"Wait!" Ophelia warned, holding out her hands in caution. It was too much of a coincidence that somebody was here now, and her heart raced as suspicion set in. She crept quietly to the window, drew back the lace curtain…

And paled. Leonard and Hector stood on the porch, shifting impatiently as they knocked again.

"It's them," Ophelia whispered, her voice cracking with fear. How the hell had they found her? "It's the men who want the sapphire."

The color drained from Luce's face, but Enid only furrowed

her brow. "Here?"

"Yes, here, standing at your bloody doorstep." Ophelia glanced around, eyeing the backdoor. The fields were so open that they wouldn't be hidden for long, no matter their escape route. "We need to hide."

"The pantry cupboard," Enid ordered, pointing at the narrow doorway between the kitchen and the living room. It was as good a place as any. Ophelia dragged Luce into it quickly, the backpack slung on one shoulder crashing into tins of baked beans and sacks of potatoes. Luce was no more elegant, swiping her hand along the shelves and sending a rack of spices toppling like dominoes.

"Bollocks!" she cursed.

Ophelia shushed her and closed the door behind them, holding her breath. She didn't realize until moments later that she was still clutching Luce's hand tightly.

She didn't let go.

Luce's own breaths were shaky and uneven, her chest heaving erratically. Ophelia squeezed and then began to trace spirals across her cold skin, along the lines of her palms and the bands of her rings. She heard the front door open, heard Enid give her visitors the same short-tempered greeting she'd given Luce and Ophelia yesterday.

"You're trespassing on private land. Get gone."

A deep clearing of a throat, and then Leonard's charming, clear voice: "We do apologize, ma'am. It's just that we're looking for two women who might have passed through here in the last day or so."

"Nobody passes through here," Enid said. "If they did, my dog would have their hand off."

Ophelia stifled a laugh despite herself, her spine pressing

painfully into the uneven shelves behind.

"Oh… er, right," Leonard said. Ophelia could almost imagine him dithering in the doorway. He was a decent professor and an even better mentor, but Ophelia saw through that now and was quite certain he was also a coward. "It's just, it's very important, you see…."

"Ophelia." Luce's whisper distracted Ophelia from the conversation, and she swiveled her head to find Luce's jaw clenched, her lips pursed as though she were in pain.

"What?"

Luce pointed, and then her face scrunched and she tore her hand away to wipe her nose. Ophelia only understood when Luce shook with a silent sneeze. A dense cloud of paprika had escaped its pot when Luce had knocked the spice rack, and it tickled Ophelia's nose as Luce trapped another sneeze.

"No," she whispered, and then, when Luce sneezed again, "No!" She pinched Luce's nose just as Luce let out an almighty "*Achoo!*" Not only did it echo through the pantry, but the sneeze sprayed all over Ophelia's hand.

Grimacing, she wiped it on her coat. "*Luce!*" she scolded in a whisper.

"It got in my nose! I couldn't help it!"

Ophelia opened her mouth to make a retort, but she didn't get a chance. The pantry door squeaked open on old hinges. Leonard waited on the other side. A lopsided smile unfolded on his thin lips, and he pushed his glasses further onto the bridge of his nose. "Hello, Ophelia. Fancy seeing you here."

Ophelia was frozen and too aware of the weight of the ring in her pocket, the ring she couldn't let go of now. She shuffled further back, pots and tins clattering against her hulking backpack.

And then Luce screamed, "Run!" as she shook the jar of orange spice into Leonard's eyes, creating another ominous cloud of paprika.

Adrenaline pushed Ophelia forward. She clutched Luce's arm for dear life and dragged her away from the pantry to the front door, catching a glimpse of Enid on her way out.

"Thank you again, Enid! Goodbye!"

They sprinted through the threshold together, Ophelia pushing straight past Hector, who had been loitering on the porch.

"Oy!" Hector shouted. A sudden resistance tugged Ophelia backward, and she looked over her shoulder to find him gripping Luce's hand. His features drew together and Luce cried out when his knuckles whitened with force.

"She has the ring!" he shouted. "She's bloody wearing it, stupid sod!"

Ophelia didn't have time to understand. She rushed back and kneed Hector in the groin, and then they were running again hand in hand, half of Enid's shed and kitchen jostling up and down on her back as she dragged Luce toward the fringe of forest awaiting them. She didn't dare look to see if they were following. As long as Luce was by her side, nothing else mattered.

They ran until Ophelia's calves burned and the sky above them was fragmented by branches and treetops. And even then, when Ophelia could barely breathe, they didn't stop running. Not until they were sure they were safe again.

Chapter Nine

"I need… to stop," Luce gasped out. They'd gone straight from running to climbing uphill, and while she had no desire to run into the men after them again, she could no longer find enough strength in her legs to carry her forward.

Ophelia glanced around and then gestured upward, past a scattering of pines. "I can see some rocks up there. Just a bit more."

"*Ugh.*"

She grabbed Luce's hands roughly and yanked. Apparently, Luce's dignity had dwindled with her energy, because she let her — all the way to the top of the incline, where a cluster of rocks and boulders sat beneath a craggy cliff top.

Luce collapsed onto the half-frozen soil and slumped against the rocks, sucking in as much cool air as she could. Her entire body protested against the amount of work it had taken her, the aches only settling into her joints as her adrenaline ebbed.

Ophelia fell next to her, unzipping her backpack and pulling out a bottle of water.

"Do you happen to have a gurney in there?" asked Luce. "You're going to need one if you want to take me any further."

Ophelia wrinkled her nose and gulped down half of the water before handing it to Luce. "I believe that's one of the few things Enid didn't think to pack."

"Shouldn't we call the police or something?"

"Well, we don't have a phone for starters. And what would we tell them, anyway? 'Two con men have been chasing us through the mountains, but it's okay because they only want a hundred-year-old artifact I stole from a museum.'"

"Fair point." Luce nodded, unzipping her coat slightly to cool herself down. "So what do we do now?"

"They can't be far behind. We have to keep going if we want to make it to the lake before them. Come on." Ophelia wobbled back onto her feet slowly and extended a hand.

Wide-eyed, Luce almost choked on her own disbelief. "Sorry, what?"

Ophelia frowned and let her arm fall to her side. "What?"

"I'm not coming with you, Indiana Jones! You promised me you'd take me back to the lodge, not drag me on the run with you — *again*."

A flicker of something solemn, something like disappointment, passed across Ophelia's features with the low winter sun. "But that was before!" she stuttered. "And they think you have the ring! They've seen your face clearly now. Even if you go back, you're not safe."

"No." Luce shook her head and swallowed down her rising panic, somehow managing to hoist herself back up onto her jelly-like legs. "No, I'm not doing this again. I'll find my own bloody way back."

"Luce...." Ophelia sighed as Luce began to stride away. "Luce, hang on. Think about this."

"I *am* thinking about this! I've been thinking about it nonstop since you took my canoe on a bloody joyride! I have things to get back to, Ophelia." Luce's mouth turned dry and gritty, the taste of something rotten clinging to her tongue. "I'm not cut out for your silly little quest! I have bigger things to worry about than a chuffing ring and an imaginary curse!"

Ophelia recoiled as though her words had been a physical slap to the face, and beneath the humming anxiety in Luce's veins, she felt a spark of guilt waiting to paralyze her.

She closed her eyes and took as deep a breath as her lungs could manage. "I'm sorry. I know this is important to you, and I understand... I think. But I'm not like you, Ophelia. I can't just grab my hat and whip and run off to do my thing. I..."

Luce couldn't find the words to explain, not without confessing the truth: that she was a mess. An anxious, weak, sad mess. That she was a slave to the thoughts in her head and that the simplest of tasks felt like a higher mountain to climb than the one she stood on now. That she needed those antidepressants still in her cabin or else it would only get worse.

"You what, Luce?" Ophelia's voice softened, and then her hands were in Luce's, their noses inches apart. "Tell me. It's okay. You can tell me."

Luce shook her head even as tears pricked her eyes. She couldn't. It wasn't that easy. It had never been that easy.

"We can figure it out together if you just tell me," Ophelia murmured. The pad of her thumb swiped across the damp tears rolling down Luce's wind-slapped cheeks.

"I..." Luce hated how weak she sounded, her voice trembling like a child's. She bit down on her bottom lip to keep it from wobbling and tried to force out the words. But they wouldn't come. They were too much of an admission, too much of a weakness, and Luce couldn't set them free yet.

Ophelia sighed, her shoulders slumping. She opened her mouth as though to say more, but Luce never found out what.

The sound of footsteps cracking through twigs and bodies rustling through underbrush distracted them.

Ophelia startled, her face paling and her hand rising instinctively to her coat pocket, where Luce suspected the ring must be. Luce realized that even if she had a choice, she couldn't leave her now. At least if they got it to the lake, everything she'd endured would be worth it. Maybe she *was* in too deep to turn back. And even if she wasn't, where would she go? Ophelia was right. Those men thought she had the ring. They were after her, too.

"That's them," Ophelia said, panic dancing in her eyes. "We have to go."

Reluctantly, Luce nodded and took Ophelia's outstretched hand, readying herself for more running and struggling. But that was just what she did every day, whether she was sitting on her sofa at home or working at the law firm or here. And at least here she was with Ophelia.

As the footsteps neared, Ophelia pulled her away from the rocks, her backpack slapping against her spine. They set off into a run again, and Luce was just glad for the plasters covering her blistered heels and the dry clothes Enid had provided them.

They wove their way further into the mountains, and Luce only realized then that her thoughts were quieter when she was busy trying not to be caught by thieves and con men; quieter when she was with Ophelia.

She held on to that and kept going.

* * *

"We must have lost them by now, surely," Ophelia breathed, finally slowing down. Other than a break for lunch, it was the first time she'd allowed herself to stop since this morning, with Luce trailing behind looking worn. Loose strands of her dark hair stuck to her neck with the sweat, lines carving themselves along the dark stains beneath her eyes, and she was gasping. There was no way she'd get much further tonight, and Ophelia didn't dare drag her.

Besides, the sun was sinking into the mountains, and hiking in the dark wouldn't get them very far. Ophelia slid out of the heavy backpack, sighing in relief when her shoulders were no longer breaking under its weight. She pulled out the atlas Enid had kindly packed for her and flicked to the page centered on this part of the Highlands, with High Mór a small dot on the peak of the grassy mountains. Ophelia calculated that they were about halfway there, which meant if they moved as quickly tomorrow, they could reach the lake by dusk — providing Leonard didn't find them first. She hadn't seen or heard anybody trailing them since this morning, and that gave her hope.

Luce had already collapsed onto the ground, wetting her dry lips as she sucked in the fresh air. "If I ever get home, I'm going to devour so much pizza. I've earned it."

A fond smile tugged at the corner of Ophelia's mouth, a strange wave of warmth flooding her. She'd waited for Luce to complain all day, to tell her that she was going back with or without Ophelia, but somehow, Luce had stayed. And though it was selfish of Ophelia, she was glad.

"Pizza's on me." Ophelia hauled out the sleeping bags and the tent next, the pegs scattering out onto the floor. "I owe you a lifetime supply."

"Far more than that," Luce muttered, but for once, her words weren't sharp with scorn.

A laugh bubbled in Ophelia as she glanced at Luce and remembered the way she had thrown paprika in Leonard's face. Ophelia might have made an awful mess of everything, but she'd found herself having fun, enjoying it. It reminded her of old adventures with university friends, or her days of traveling with Peter — only more real, somehow, because the memories wouldn't be sun-soaked or picture-perfect. They would be messy and grimy with soil and darkened by clouds in the way the best memories always were.

And they would feature Luce: Luce propping herself up on a boulder, water dribbling down her chin as she drained the last of today's supplies; Luce pointing out an owl perched in one of the trees, only for Ophelia to inform her that it was actually a hawk; Luce, looking at her with eyes the color of rain-kissed leaves, and smiling as though maybe they were friends, as though maybe she liked Ophelia beneath all of that hostility.

Ophelia tried to distract herself from her thoughts of Luce by hammering the pegs into the marshy soil. Her fingers were numb from the cold, but lighting a fire tonight would pose the risk of Leonard finding them.

"Could you pass me one of the poles?" Ophelia asked, swiping her clammy palms down her thermal trousers as she straightened.

Luce did, extending the tent pole toward Ophelia. Ophelia took it, pausing without meaning to when she caught the silver gleam on Luce's finger. The ring. It was the first time she'd gotten a proper look at it. Perhaps to anyone who hadn't spent every day for the last three years working next to Eilidh's ring, they did look similar, though Luce's sapphire was clean-cut and more vibrant than the cloudy, midnight-blue Hebridean one of Eilidh's.

Ophelia couldn't help it. She dropped the pole and pulled Luce's hand closer so that she could examine it properly. "Where did you get it? The ring, I mean."

Luce's pinky finger twitched against Ophelia's palm. "It was just a birthday gift from my mum. Sapphire is my birthstone."

"It is *quite* similar to Eilidh's. I can see how an untrained eye might mistake it for hers." Narrowing her eyes, Ophelia dropped Luce's hand and went back to building the tent. Still, the ghost of Luce's touch burned her palms, branding her, and she almost wished she would have found an excuse to keep it for a few moments longer.

"Oh, God," Luce said as Ophelia assembled the third and fourth poles. "I'm going to have to wee in a bush, aren't I?"

Ophelia wrinkled her nose. She'd come to the same realization at lunch and it hadn't been pleasant. "I'm afraid so."

A sigh as Luce contemplated this before placing down her water bottle and crossing her arms. "I can't believe some people actually do this for fun." She was already marching off into the bushes, and Ophelia couldn't help but smirk.

By the time Luce returned, Ophelia had finished assembling the tent. She gazed upon her work proudly before unrolling the sleeping bags inside. She'd slept in far worse places.

When she looked up, though, she found Luce pale and gazing at something past Ophelia. She picked at her nails absently, looking more like an apparition than a real person.

"Luce? You okay?"

Luce's eyes snapped back into focus as she nodded and hummed an unconvincing "Uh-huh." Still, her breath came out ragged and she wouldn't meet Ophelia's eye.

Once again, guilt crawled through Ophelia and she wondered what it was that Luce wasn't saying. What it was that she'd been about to say this morning when they'd heard Leonard approaching. She'd been ready to leave then. Was she going to leave now instead?

But Luce only crouched and scrambled through the backpack. "Just hungry," she said.

Ophelia didn't believe her, but she didn't dare pry either.

* * *

Luce couldn't sleep — again. Her relentless fidgeting was annoying even her, never mind Ophelia, who lay peacefully in the sleeping bag beside her. On top of her usual anxiety, she was once again listening out for the sound of bears or wolves or some other wild animal that could very well kill her if it wanted.

And she was thinking of home. She was thinking of her own comforts: the blanket she wrapped herself in when she was cold, the film she watched when no other distraction would work, the sound of her mother spilling the latest drama about the scandalous ladies she went to book club with over the phone. She was thinking of her medication, and how it had been almost three days without it. Three days without the chemicals she needed to keep her even a little bit balanced. She had constant brain zaps now every time she moved, like head rushes but with electricity, and everything felt foggy, like she was a zombie trapped in a huge vat of tar. Moving was harder. Thinking was harder. Everything was harder.

"You can talk to me, you know." Ophelia's words startled Luce, though they were said gently enough.

Luce pulled her sleeping bag to cover her shoulders, kicking out her restless legs. "About what?"

"Anything. Whatever's bothering you. You listened to me about the curse and about Peter. You can trust me to listen to you, too."

It was easy for Ophelia to say that. She didn't know what she was promising, didn't know what she was getting into. Luce had trusted people with her anxiety before. She'd asked for help from her general practitioner three times before they'd listened for long enough to put her on medication and refer her to a counselor. She'd told her mum before that, and her mum had dismissed her with: "It's probably just hormones. Is it that time of the month?"

And then there were the friends who had grown tired of her and had stopped inviting her anywhere, or the ones Luce just hadn't had the energy to maintain contact with when she was only trying to keep her head above water. There was her boss, who never gave her time off work unless she came in with an awful case of the flu. There were her past relationships, a string of failed attempts at trying to be normal, trying to *have* normal, when she just wasn't — because antidepressants lowered her sex drive and because even if they didn't, her stress-induced stomachaches and fatigue meant she was rarely in the mood, and because eating in restaurants made her feel trapped and going on nice holidays and city breaks was a chore rather than a pleasure.

It was why she had stopped talking about her anxiety in the end. Therapy and counseling hadn't helped. The pills just about kept her going. She couldn't handle another person recommending she try yoga or apple-picking or living on a diet of avocados. She couldn't handle another person not understanding.

A tear rolled from the corner of Luce's eye, dripping onto her knobbly pillow, and she was glad for the darkness of the tent. She didn't even know what to say. If she talked now, Ophelia would surely hear the lump clogging her throat.

"Luce?"

She heard Ophelia move, didn't dare turn around.

"Well, I know you're not asleep, because you haven't slept at all since I've met you. I'm beginning to suspect that you're a vampire, actually. Which I don't have a problem with, by the way. I had quite the crush on Alice Cullen in my—"

"It's anxiety." The words spilled from Luce before she could stop them. She didn't even know why. It felt like a betrayal, one committed by her own tongue, and she bit down on it as though that might take the words back.

But they were out there now, floating between them, and the only thing protecting Luce was the fact that she had her back turned and the sleeping bag pulled up to her neck.

Silence blanketed them for a while. Not long enough.

Ophelia whispered, "I'm so sorry, Luce. I didn't know. Do you get panic attacks?"

Luce shrugged. "It's more constant than just panic attacks. Generalized anxiety disorder is the technical term, but... I don't know. I don't understand it myself half the time."

"Are you..."

Luce heard Ophelia swallow and she squeezed her eyes closed, hating every moment of this vulnerability. She was still waiting for one of the silly questions, the unsolicited advice, the implication that it was all in her head even though Luce could feel it coiling through every bone in her body, every organ, every cell.

"Are you anxious now?"

"I'm always anxious. Sometimes I notice it less, but it's always there. Worse because I haven't taken my antidepressants. Withdrawals make me foggy and on edge."

"What can I do?" Ophelia's voice was earth-shatteringly soft, and somehow it felt like the beginning of everything. If the world ended with a whimper, it started with this whisper, here, now; it started with Ophelia and her softness and her strangeness and the secrets shared in this tent, and Luce could feel it. It was turning her walls to ash, weakening her strength. "How can I help?"

Luce frowned and forced herself to turn around. She found Ophelia resting on her elbow, concern swimming in her eyes as she waited for an answer — an answer Luce didn't have. Nobody had ever asked how to help before. They'd told her how to help herself — exercise, diet, meditation — but nobody had ever taken it upon themselves to try to support her like Ophelia was now.

Trying not to choke on the lump in her throat, Luce said, "I... I don't know."

"Is there anything I can do to take your mind off things? Anything that makes you feel calmer?"

Luce could only shake her head and try not to dissolve into tears. She felt so fragile, so childlike, tucked into a sleeping bag while Ophelia leaned over her, trying to help her, but for once, the raw openness didn't feel like a burden. For once, it felt like a comfort.

"Could I... could I try something?"

Luce hesitated for only a moment before nodding.

"Give me your hand," Ophelia murmured.

Luce pulled it out of the sleeping bag and extended it to Ophelia, her heart thrumming wildly. Soft fingertips found her palm a moment later, Ophelia nothing more than a silhouette of untamed hair in the darkness. She swirled her fingernail into Luce's palm and then rolled up her sleeve. Goosebumps chased her touch, always one step behind, as Ophelia carved shapes into Luce's bare arm. She started with the hard bone of her wrist and then turned over to the fleshy, thin skin beneath. Luce twitched when she found the sensitive part of her inner elbow, dancing along creases and invisible veins, reminding Luce of the parts of her she never usually noticed.

And it distracted her for just long enough that she forgot that she was drowning. Instead, she floated on the surface for a while, a place she never usually got to see.

"I'm sorry for dragging you into this, Luce. I really am. If I'd have known…"

"I'm not," Luce replied too quickly. "I'm not sorry."

If she hadn't been dragged into this, she wouldn't have met Ophelia. She wouldn't have found the bravery to throw paprika into a man's face. She wouldn't have had this moment, now, which was infinitely better and infinitely more intimate than anything she'd ever experienced before. She was afraid and she was crawling in her skin and she was trying to survive every second as it passed, but she was here, and she wasn't sorry, and she didn't want Ophelia to be, either.

"Tell me if you want me to stop." Ophelia lowered onto her side with Luce's arm between them, still tracing a new language onto Luce's skin. It left her relaxed enough that she yawned, exhaustion suddenly pressing on her like bricks.

"S'nice," Luce managed to say in the haze of her tiredness. "Don't stop."

She felt Ophelia's eyes on her as her own lids shuttered and sleep claimed her, her skin still buzzing and itching and dancing with Ophelia's touch. And she was in a tent with a woman who'd been a stranger not so long ago, and she was frightened, and she didn't know what tomorrow would bring, and yet she still wasn't sorry.

She didn't think she'd ever be sorry.

Chapter Ten

"Luce."

Luce groaned when her peaceful sleep was disrupted by the sound of her name being whispered. With her eyes closed, she couldn't quite remember where she was or who could be talking to her. She lived alone. But her comfortable memory-foam mattress had flattened to something hard and lumpy beneath her spine, and something too close by was dripping loudly.

"*Luce,*" the strange voice called more urgently.

And then reality rushed back all at once. She fluttered her eyes open slowly and was greeted by the sage-green nylon of the tent wall. Watery light bounced off the other side, casting shadows of rain droplets that dappled Luce's face. She grumbled again and threw her arm over her eyes, another day of hiking and being chased too daunting to contemplate.

"*Luuuuce,*" Ophelia singsonged now, her fingernail tracing across Luce's eyebrows. Luce scrunched her face. It tickled. "Oh no. Is that a *wolf*?"

Chapter Ten

"What?" Luce shot up so quickly that the world tilted, searching for the wild animal. From here, she could only see Ophelia sitting by the tent's opening, wreathed in the hazy morning mist behind her. "Where?"

Ophelia's lips snaked into an amused smirk before she pressed a finger to them. "Shh. Look." She gestured to something outside the tent, something Luce couldn't see.

Still wary, Luce slowly crawled to the opening beside Luce, their arms brushing. Her warmth was a relief, and the sharp smell of the mountain's wild clung to her, earthy and reminding Luce of rain. She peered out in the direction Ophelia was pointing and tried not to acknowledge the embarrassment churning through her at the memory of last night. She'd shared too much of herself. Now she couldn't hide behind her bitter quips and well-put-together appearance the way she did with everybody else. Then again, under the circumstances, she never had been able to. Not with Ophelia.

Then she gasped when, squinting, she made out a silhouette rustling through dead leaves and murky tendrils of thick fog. Four slender legs came into view first, and then the sharp antlers of a stag brushing the ground as he grazed, oblivious to their presence. Luce had never seen anything like it, and her heart stopped, froze, restarted. She spent most of her life among criminals and fraudsters and snooty coworkers in the city, always deafened by blaring car horns and ringing phones. She'd forgotten that there was a world outside of that. She'd forgotten that peace could exist — for the world and for herself.

But it was here, stirring delicately with the stag, and floating between Luce and Ophelia as they watched in awed silence.

"Isn't he beautiful?" Ophelia whispered.

Luce nodded, her eyes pricking — with tears or the cold,

she didn't know. She only knew that, for a moment, she was somewhere other than her own restless, sore body and erratic mind. For once, she didn't feel trapped or afraid. Her only job was to be calm and to observe, and she was happy to as the stag continued to forage.

Until the weight of Ophelia's gaze pinned her down. Luce turned her head to meet her eyes, to ask why she was looking at Luce when there was a majestic wild animal in front of them, but the words got lost in her throat. The way that Ophelia was looking at her... the way her blue eyes twinkled, with a ring of turquoise around the pupils...

Words would ruin it. Something bigger than speech was passing between them.

Goosebumps pebbled along Luce's skin, the tingling rising up her neck, to her cheeks, as she swallowed against a dry mouth. Ophelia's eyes drifted down just slightly to Luce's lips.

For the first time in her life, Luce didn't think. She let her body urge her forward, toward Ophelia, knowing that was where it should be. Close to her. Like it had been all night, while Ophelia had touched her skin as though she were a sacred, centuries-old scroll of fragile parchment. Their noses brushed. Luce's heart thrashed against her ribcage with anticipation, with need. She hadn't *needed* like this in a long time. Her days were spent just trying to survive; she hadn't had room for anything else.

But she had it now, suddenly. An area usually filled by exhaustion and dread seemed to have cleared to make room for Ophelia. And Luce wanted to fill it.

She closed the sliver of space between them.

Their lips grazed for less than a moment before Ophelia pulled away, flushed and wide-eyed. "I... I can't."

Chapter Ten

Luce's cheeks burned with humiliation as she sank back onto her heels. Of course not. Ophelia wasn't here to kiss Luce. Ophelia was here to remove a curse that she believed had taken her fiancé from her. She was here to find love again — but not with Luce.

"Sorry. I, er, I don't know what I was think—"

Her words came to an abrupt halt, a sudden rustle of movement distracting her. The stag scurried away as though something had startled it, its white rear the last thing Luce saw before it disappeared into the mist.

"*Shit*," Ophelia cursed. "It's them. We have to go."

Luce frowned, and then a pang of fear lanced through her when she saw the distant shadows of two men approaching. They'd found them.

She kicked her feet out of the sleeping bag and pulled her shoes on quickly, Ophelia doing the same before shoving whatever she could manage back into the backpack. "We don't have time to take the rest. Come on."

Luce scrambled to stand and followed Ophelia out of the tent. Her panic only worsened when she saw the men were closer now, almost where the stag had been standing. Ophelia grabbed her hand and pulled her forward.

"Come on, Luce."

She stumbled forward on unfeeling legs as they broke into a run, heading up a muddy trail into the mountains. Luce could just about make out the thick trunks of the silver birches as she weaved through them, tripping over her own feet as she did. She didn't know how long they continued on, the fog freezing itself in her lungs and the crescent moon still visible in dawn's pale-blue sky. When she looked over her shoulder, she found no sign of Leonard or Hector behind her.

The distraction made her clumsy, though, and her foot caught in a raised tree root before twisting awkwardly at the ankle. Luce yelped out against the sharp pain, losing her balance and toppling over. She gripped desperately at weeds and soil and dead grass as she began to slip, but gravity wasn't on her side, and she ended up tumbling down the uneven, rocky incline at a bruising speed, disoriented and desperately seeking Ophelia, who was calling her name somewhere distant. *Too* distant.

Finally, when Luce's bones were tender and aching nausea was whirling in her gut, she rolled to a stop on flatter ground, tucked into the fetal position and not daring to move.

"Luce!" Ophelia's call came from above. "Luce, are you okay?"

Grimacing, Luce stretched out her legs first, and when only a dull pain shot through her shin, she unraveled herself completely — only to freeze again, flat on her back, as icy fear flooded through her.

The gray-haired man who had been a victim of the paprika yesterday peered down at her through round, condensation-fogged glasses, his hands resting in his pockets and a vague, haughty look of satisfaction on his face.

"Hector. I've caught one of them," he called.

Luce's instinct was to run, but her joints wouldn't put themselves back together quickly enough. By the time she was halfway to standing, a hand was pinning her against a hard, warm body. "No! Please!"

The other man — Hector — leered at her now, his upper lip curled in satisfaction. He was much broader and crueller-looking than the first, Leonard, with harsh, craggy features and greed curling across his mouth. "Let's get her somewhere hidden, shall we? See how willing she is to talk after she's been tied up and gagged for a while."

"*Oph*—" Luce's scream was muffled by Leonard's grimy hand, and then she was being shoved forward. She tried desperately to elbow Leonard in the ribs, but his hot breath filled the shell of her ear with a whisper: "Would you rather me or him? I don't want to hurt you."

She stilled. Leonard had a point. He was the lesser of two evils, if she was any good at judging people — and she hoped, after so long working in law, that she was.

"Good girl," Leonard muttered, loosening his grip. "Now, I'm no happier about this than you are. But you have something that Hector wants, and unfortunately, we've all been dragged into his games. Play nicely, and I'll get you back to Ophelia before you can say… oh, I don't know, 'porridge and honey.' Yes?"

Luce nodded, her eyes flooding with tears. She looked to the spot she had just landed on, desperate to be saved — but Ophelia was nowhere to be seen, and she was being dragged too quickly. Soon she'd be lost, and how would she ever find Ophelia again in the middle of nowhere?

"I don't know where the sapphire is," she said, her voice cracking.

Hector turned around and grinned, a flash of a golden canine winking in the light. "We'll see about that, shall we?"

* * *

Hector bound Luce's wrists together with rope. He'd snatched her ring from her finger before she'd even had time to tell him that it wasn't the one he was looking for — and if he was stupid enough not to know the difference, perhaps that was his problem, so she didn't bother now. Instead, she sat in a soggy, muddy puddle in a shallow cliff cave, the sound of rainwater dripping an inconvenient reminder of how desperate she was for a wee. Again.

Leonard paced behind Hector, chewing the nib of his glasses and scraping his greasy, graying hair off his face. Luce was beginning to believe that he'd meant what he'd said: in his torn tweed blazer and scuffed brogues, he didn't exactly look the sort to find a thrill in kidnapping and theft.

Hector, on the other hand, kept grinning at Luce as though she were a rasher of bacon sizzling in a frying pan and he a starving dog. She glared at him. She refused to be afraid of a man named Hector — if, of course, that was really his name. Either way, she wouldn't give him the satisfaction. If her anxiety disorder had taught her anything, it was how to look fiercely calm and composed on the outside while her insides disintegrated into puddles of fear and panic.

"All right, love," Hector began, his voice a rough rasp. His boots squelched in a puddle as he knelt in front of Luce and tied her ankles together, too. She winced when the rough rope chafed painfully against her skin. "I'll forgive you and your friend of the damage you did to my nether regions yesterday if you tell me where to find more of these sapphires."

"I told you I don't know," Luce ground out. "I have nothing to do with any of this."

The air was stolen from her lungs when Hector pinned her to the cold, uneven stone wall by her neck, his forearm pressing on her windpipe until she wheezed. Her scalp stung from the sudden impact. "Let's try again."

"Hector," Leonard tutted. "Must we resort to violence? If she says she doesn't know, she doesn't know."

"Bullshit." Hector's saliva sprayed across Luce's face, and she squeezed her eyes shut to protect herself. "She knows. She's working with your lass. Why else would they be together?"

"She stole my canoe," Luce forced out, coughing as she did. Maybe now, heaving in any scrap of air she could find, she was a little bit afraid. "I got caught up in all of this by accident."

Hector pressed harder, until Luce could only whimper and claw Hector's elbow in vain with her bound hands. "I'll ask once more, and then I'm going to get impatient. You wouldn't like to see me impatient. Where. Is. The. Lake?"

"Hector, please," Leonard begged now, stretching a hand out uselessly. "Be careful."

Luce was released without warning. She slumped, coughing against the burning in her throat, her lungs. Hector had hopped up and whipped around to Leonard, jabbing a stubby finger into Leonard's shoulder. "*You* said she'd lead us to the lake. That was the deal. If I don't get what I asked for, Green, I swear to God—"

"All right." Leonard lifted his hands in surrender, stuttering out, "Calm down, *please*. I said that Ophelia would lead us to the lake. Not whoever this is. I've never even seen her before. I daresay she may not even be an archaeologist."

"I'm not!" Luce shouted.

"Use your head, Professor." Hector gave three rough taps to Leonards temple. "She had the ring!"

"Maybe it was a gift," Leonard replied. "Maybe she and Ophelia are... partners in another way."

Hector only scoffed and returned his focus to Luce. His dark eyes sparkled with threat, his hands fisted at his sides. "I don't care if she's married to the Queen of bloody England. She'll tell me where that lake is... and if she doesn't, we'll find it ourselves and throw her in. See how she likes that."

Luce shuddered, Hector's low threat crawling like spiders across her skin. He narrowed his eyes and thrust his hand into his pocket before pulling out a penknife and brandishing it at her. The small silver blade grinned like a set of sparkling teeth, and all of Luce's hope and resolve wilted at once.

There was a chance she wasn't getting out of Scotland alive.

Bloody Juliet and her bloody adventure holiday. Why couldn't she have just booked a spa? Nobody would have tried to kill her at a spa... she hoped.

Chapter Eleven

"Luce!" Ophelia had been screaming her name at the top of her lungs for at least twenty minutes. By the time she'd found a safe way of descending the steep slope Luce had tumbled down, Luce had disappeared, and it had left Ophelia trembling with panic. Now she couldn't find Luce anywhere. What if she was lost? What if she was hurt? What if she'd fallen again, or what if Leonard had found her?

Worst of all, what if it was the curse again? Ophelia had been so careful. She'd wanted nothing more than to kiss Luce this morning, but she hadn't let herself for fear that Eilidh's curse would touch her.

And now it had anyway. Luce was gone.

Ophelia stifled a sob as she continued her search, trying not to notice the cliff's edge not too far from where Luce had fallen. She couldn't have fallen any further. Ophelia had heard her shout after the tumble. She'd heard her *here*. So where had she gone?

"Luce!" Ophelia's scream was raw and thick with tears as she

marched on and on, and —

There. There, in the damp soil, among snapped twigs and flattened leaves, was an imprint of a boot. Someone had been here, and it had been this morning, after the frost had thawed.

Hope rekindled in Ophelia's gut. She followed the tracks closely, desperate not to miss one. She'd managed to find Eilidh's ring buried in the silt of the lake. She could find Luce. She could.

She would.

Muffled murmurs suddenly floated from somewhere nearby. Ophelia glanced around for the source, a shiver of fear rolling down her spine when a low, familiar voice reached her. Leonard. Hector's rasp followed.

And then Luce whimpering, pleading with them, telling them that she didn't know where the lake was. The sounds came from a shallow cave within the craggy rocks not too far from where Ophelia stood.

Hatred coiled like an adder in her gut, but also, worse than that, guilt. They'd taken Luce, maybe even *hurt* her, because Ophelia had prioritized the ring. She'd dragged Luce into all of this. Ophelia couldn't bear to think of what awful things Hector and Leonard might be doing to her now.

She crept toward the entrance of the cave, trying to steady her breathing.

"I don't care if she's married to the Queen of bloody England. She'll tell me where that lake is… and if she doesn't, we'll find it ourselves and throw her in. See how she likes that." The voice was Hector's, a low snarl that left Ophelia nauseous. She heard him shuffle on heavy feet and imagined him trying to harm Luce.

She couldn't let him.

98

She pushed off the rocks and entered the cave, her hands lifted in surrender. A penknife was pointed in her direction, gripped by Hector. Leonard stood looking flustered and pathetic in the shadows, and on the other side of the cave, damp and trembling, was Luce. They'd tied her up, both her wrists and her ankles, but relief seemed to dance in her tear-filled eyes when Ophelia glanced at her. She searched for any sign of injury and was glad to find none.

"Ophelia?" Leonard muttered. He had the audacity to look surprised — regretful, even.

Hector only grinned.

"I'll take you to the lake." Somehow, Ophelia summoned the courage to look Hector in the eyes. They were cold and dark and wicked: the eyes of a man she'd never trust. But she didn't have a choice now. "I know where it is. I can take you."

Hector cocked his head. "Why now?"

"Because I won't let anybody get hurt for a few gemstones. It isn't worth it."

"Seems you were right, Leonard." Hector motioned between Ophelia and Luce with his knife and wiggled his brows. "Partners."

Ophelia frowned. Did they think she and Luce were working together? That Luce was Ophelia's accomplice?

Either way, Leonard only pursed his lips and let out a ragged sigh. He kept his head bowed, eyes to the floor, as he said, "Let's just get this done with, Hector. Enough's enough."

"Couldn't agree more." Hector crouched and sawed through the rope binding Luce's ankles, causing both her and Ophelia to wince. Then he stood, tugging Luce up, too, and gestured forward invitingly. "Lead the way, love. I'll take care of your friend until we get there."

Ophelia swallowed down the acidic bile gathering in her throat and readied herself for the hike. "Off we go, then."

Chapter Twelve

~⟨ formatted ornament ⟩~

Daylight still lingered when Ophelia brought the group to a stop before a set of burbling waterfalls. The rippling lake was a desaturated gray in the fog, kissing the low-hanging clouds curling around the peaks of the mountains.

It wasn't Eilidh's lake — but Hector and Leonard were none the wiser. Luce had filled Ophelia in on the fact that they had mistaken her sapphire ring for Eilidh's, just as they had on Enid's farm, and it had given Ophelia the confidence to take them somewhere else, somewhere that they would believe was the place the ring had been found.

Judging from the gleeful avarice twisting across Hector's features, it had worked.

A sadness sifted through Ophelia with the wind, happier memories of a time before the curse resurfacing. She'd been to these pools before, with Peter. It had been summer, not long after he'd proposed, and they'd been brave enough to wash in the lake together on a hike through the Hebrides. It had been one of the best days of her life. They'd kissed under the waterfalls, half-naked and cold and in love. Ophelia missed him so much that her heart tightened and she had to force her breathing to remain even. If nothing else, this place was another reminder of why she needed to get to High Mór and lift the curse — so that she would never have to love and then lose again. So that she could give her heart away without worrying about the repercussions, just as she had wanted to with Luce this morning.

"This is it?" Hector questioned, yanking Luce forward. Her hands were still bound, her jaw clenched, and another pang of pain jolted through Ophelia at the fact. She just wanted Luce to be safe and okay. She should never have dragged her into this.

Leonard had stopped beside Ophelia, and he swiped his glasses off to take in the view. "It's beautiful."

Ophelia nodded, blank, empty. "This is where I found the ring," she lied. "Are we done here?"

Hector narrowed his eyes, causing Ophelia to stiffen. Glancing around a final time, he pulled out his penknife.

Panic flooding her, Ophelia leaped with her fear toward him and Luce, whose face had a ghastly pallor. "Stop! I did what you asked!"

"Relax, love." Hector raised his hands as though in surrender, the penknife steady in his hand. His nails were chewed down to the quick and caked with grime. Ophelia wondered how she hadn't suspected him from the beginning. "I'm only cutting her free."

Relieved, she took a step back. Her back collided with Leonard's torso, the smell of stale, expensive cologne and tobacco washing over her from his tattered blazer. She whipped around, the anger she had kept behind a tightly locked gate for days finally seeping through. Leonard had been her mentor, her tutor, perhaps even her friend. He'd taught her everything she knew. He'd answered her frantic emails about deadlines and field trips at three o'clock in the morning and he'd gotten her her first work placement, the one that had led to her career in history, archaeology, and curation. And now he was here, helping a con man steal an artifact, threatening Luce. Ophelia still understood none of it: he was still Leonard, still awkward and kind-faced and soft-spoken, and yet, somehow, he'd been capable of all of this.

It was the betrayal that stung the most. Ophelia glared up at him, despising the way his eyebrows knitted together with pity. "I thought you were better than this."

"I didn't want any of this, Ophelia," he replied. "I swear it. I never meant to cause you any harm, physical or otherwise."

"Then why?"

Leonard's eyes flickered to Hector, something sharp and hostile guttering in them, and Ophelia only then wondered for the first time whether he was just as much a pawn in Hector's game of greed as everyone else here. "The offer wasn't one I could refuse."

Ophelia lowered her voice. "Why? What's he holding over you?"

"I needed the money." A sigh, troubled and thick with pain. Leonard slipped his glasses back on as though they were his shield, staring out at the falls. His face was smeared with dirt, just as Ophelia imagined hers was, and his throat bobbed with a swallow. "My son is ill. He needs a surgery that's only offered by a surgeon in America. My savings aren't enough to cover the trip *and* the procedure, and if he doesn't go... he's only twelve,

Ophelia. He deserves a chance. We were preparing ourselves for the worst when Hector turned up at the university, offering me more than enough to get Jack his treatment overseas — if I helped him track down the rare stones he needed. He knew that I'd spent my life's research on Skye's history, and he told me about the sapphire. That was when I remembered Eilidh's ring, how you told me you'd retrieved it for an exhibition not so long ago."

Ophelia remembered sending that email. It had been the first real artifact she'd found — the first confirmation that Eilidh wasn't just a cautionary tale but a real, flesh-and-blood woman. She'd only wanted her mentor to be proud of her. Instead he'd passed on the information to a thief, a con man.

And yet she couldn't find it in her to be angry. To hate him. Leonard loved his family. They'd been his laptop screensaver, projected on the huge screen in front of hundreds of students during lectures. He'd always gushed about how his son, Jack, wanted to be an archaeologist like his father. Now, he might not get the chance.

If Ophelia had had a chance to save Peter, even if it meant doing something she wasn't proud of, she knew what choice she would have made.

She wasn't a parent. She didn't know how it must feel to risk losing a child. She didn't want to imagine it.

But Leonard wouldn't get his money if Hector didn't find the sapphires — and she doubted very much that he would here. Hector was already sniffing around the banks of the lake. Luce watched him cautiously, rubbing her wrists and grimacing.

Ophelia sighed, her morals tearing apart. She needed to lift the curse. Leonard needed the money. Was there a way to make both possible?

"This isn't Eilidh's lake," Ophelia whispered when she was sure Hector was out of earshot. "And that ring isn't Eilidh's, either. It's just a regular sapphire."

A wry smile curved across Leonard's thin lips. "I know that. I've spent my life on this island, Ophelia. Do you think I would mistake a regular sapphire for a Hebridean one?"

Ophelia frowned. "Then why—"

"Hector was going to hurt your friend," he said, his low voice turning grave as he glanced at Luce. "Honestly, I never expected to fall so deep into all of this. I've made a mess, Ophelia. I'm so terribly sorry. For all of it."

"We do what we have to." Ophelia thought of all the mistakes she'd made since this began. Stealing from the museum she worked in; dragging Luce into her problems when she had enough of her own; placing her own needs above anyone else's. The ring felt heavier than bricks in her breast pocket now. It could change Leonard's life, the life of his son, if she gave it to him.

She reached for it.

"What are you doing?" Leonard clutched her hands before she could pull it out, panicked and wide-eyed.

"You need it more than I do."

"No. No, Ophelia. I'll find another way—"

"Look what I found!" The shout interrupted Leonard's pleas, booming obnoxiously off the jutting rocks and over the running falls. They both looked over to Hector, and Ophelia had to blink to make sure that she wasn't hallucinating. Hector was grinning from ear to ear. In his hands lay a slab of blue, shimmering stone melded with dirt and rock. Sapphire. It was here, too. How had Ophelia ever missed it before?

He cheered and shoved the stone into his backpack before

continuing his search, clawing through silt and soil at the edge of the lake.

"Maybe you won't have to," Ophelia murmured in awe. "Maybe we'll both get our way."

"Imagine that." Leonard sounded just as stunned.

"Was it a lie — what you said about lifting the curse, I mean? Or was it just a way to entice me so you could get the ring for yourself?"

He blew out a long breath and rocked on his heels. "I told you that cursed relics aren't my area of expertise — but the few I've come across do imply that curses can be lifted, with either the destruction of the object or the return of it. It's worth a try."

He was right. The instruction had made perfect sense, and Ophelia had no better idea. She just hoped it worked; otherwise she had a lifetime of the curse left to manage. The thought made her glance back solemnly at Luce.

A lifetime without ever knowing what it would be like to kiss her. A lifetime wondering what could have been.

Restless and desperate to find out her fate once and for all, Ophelia wandered over to the edge of the lake and called to Hector: "Are we free to go, then?"

An overenthusiastic nod was all she got in return. Now that Hector had gotten what he'd come here for, it seemed he had no use for the rest of them.

With relief fizzing through Ophelia, she joined Luce and carefully laced their fingers together. "Are you all right?"

Luce wetted her chapped bottom lip before her green eyes landed on Ophelia. "I think so."

"We should go before he changes his mind."

She nodded, and they set off. As Ophelia passed Leonard, she bowed her head. "I hope Jack gets his surgery, Leonard."

"I hope you get rid of the curse," Leonard responded gently. Ophelia didn't know what was next for them, now: whether she'd ever be able to see her mentor as the same man she once had, or whether they'd get in touch again. Either way, she couldn't muster the energy for spite. She and Leonard were too similar for that, in their own ways. They were both just trying to fix what was broken.

It felt strange to delve back into the woods without anything anchoring her down. Her backpack was gone, no weight to haul around; Hector and Leonard were far behind them; even Luce was quiet, though her clammy hand remained in Ophelia's. After losing her this morning, Ophelia wasn't prepared to let her go.

"What now?" Luce muttered finally.

"Now we get you home."

Luce halted, and the force tugged Ophelia back, too. "But you haven't lifted the curse."

"That lake wasn't Eilidh's, Luce. I just said that to get rid of Hector. High Mór is still hours away, and I can't keep dragging you with me. Now that they're gone, I can come back alone once you're home."

"But..." Luce seemed to sputter. The protest surprised Ophelia, a line forming between her brows. Going home was what Luce had been pleading for all along, and Ophelia hadn't known why until last night. She couldn't do it anymore; she couldn't bring more harm to Luce, not now that she knew. "But we're so close. How could you just turn back now after everything we did to get here?"

Ophelia's shoulders sagged, and she inched closer to Luce, tucking a stiff strand of hair out of her green eyes so that she could better see them. They were shinier, brighter, than any sapphire or gemstone, and far more precious to Ophelia, somehow. The ring, the curse... they weren't something she could get lost in. Not like she could get lost in Luce. Almost kissing her this morning had proven that. In the end, Ophelia had to choose her. "Because you almost got hurt today, and you were already struggling. You need to get home, to your medication. I can't keep being the reason why your anxiety is worse. It isn't right. I've been so selfish, Luce. I'm so sorry."

"You didn't know," Luce whispered. Tears sparkled along her waterline. "What's a few more hours compared to the days we've already spent out here?"

"You don't even *believe* in the curse."

"I know I don't. But *you* do." Luce bit down on her bottom lip, leaning her forehead against Ophelia's. Ophelia stopped breathing. They were so close, and Ophelia felt Luce everywhere, even in the places she couldn't possibly touch: the caverns of her ribs and the knot of want tightening in her belly. She was infesting Ophelia like a living thing, burying her roots into Ophelia's soil like the trees around them, and all Ophelia wanted was to stay here and let her. But that wasn't right, cursed or not. Ophelia would sooner let the curse destroy every future relationship than let Luce suffer another moment because of her.

"Luce—"

"I want to carry on, Ophelia. It's too late to turn back." The way that Luce said it, with her eyes boring into Ophelia's... it felt as though she meant more than just their trip to High Mór. Ophelia felt the same, too. Whether they went home together now or tomorrow, Ophelia wasn't sure how she could be expected to close a door on the last few days, on the things she'd found in Luce even when she hadn't been searching.

She'd wanted to lift the curse so that she could fall in love again. Instead, it was happening in the opposite order, and that terrified her. She couldn't let the curse reach Luce as it had Peter. She wouldn't.

"It's not too late. If we set off now we could go to the nearest village and find someone willing to get you back to Alasdair Ridge. I'm sure we're only an hour or so away."

Luce's features seemed to wilt, the corners of her mouth turning down, bracketed by lines. "Why are you trying to get rid of me? Because of the kiss this morning?"

"No, of course not—"

"Well then, why?" Her voice rose, as brusque and sharp as those of the crows circling somewhere in the forest canopy. "I didn't get bloody kidnapped just so you could ditch me in the nearest village. We're almost there now. We're not turning back."

"You don't understand." Ophelia's words were strained with desperation, though she wasn't sure she even understood herself. She only knew that she was beginning to develop feelings for Luce, and as long as the curse remained, it would only end one way. She could have lived with that with anyone but Luce.

Luce shook her head. "No, I don't. I don't understand. I told you that trying to kiss you was a mistake, and it won't happen again. If you feel weird about it, just—"

"I don't feel *weird* about it!" Ophelia burst out, clutching her stomach as though it might keep the fluttering butterflies from escaping. But even if she could, her mouth couldn't trap the words quickly enough. "I feel a million things about that kiss, Luce, and weird is not one of them!"

Luce's forehead wrinkled with confusion. "What, then? What

do you feel?"

Tears dripped down Ophelia's cheeks without warning, her throat hoarse as she rasped out, "I'm cursed, Luce. I told you I'm cursed. And until I'm not, I shouldn't let myself feel anything for you. I can't let myself. I can't let the ring take anyone else away from me, especially not when I've only just gotten you."

Realization set like the sun across Luce's features, darkening her face to twilight. "*That's* why you didn't kiss me this morning?"

"Yes. That's why." Suddenly drained and exhausted, Ophelia slumped onto the nearest tree stump and rubbed at her eyes. She waited to be mocked, waited to be told she was a superstitious fool who had fallen too quickly for a woman who would never feel the same.

But Luce sighed and knelt in front of her, tilting Ophelia's chin so that they locked eyes again. "Ophelia... I'm not afraid of the curse. If you wanted to kiss me, you should have."

"But *I* am, Luce. *I'm* afraid." Ophelia's voice cracked, and she couldn't find it in her to feel embarrassed by it. "I've put you through so much; the last thing you need is to kiss somebody who's cursed."

"Why? Will I turn into a frog?"

Ophelia wrinkled her nose. "Who knows?"

"Would you still like me if I did?"

She couldn't help but snort. "Probably. It'd take more than slimy skin to put me off."

"Then I'm fine with it. Look, I know you think the curse is the reason for all of the bad things in your life, but... it's also the reason we're here." Ophelia had never heard Luce's voice so gentle. She hadn't thought her capable of it. She was always so snarky and firm and assertive. Ophelia had liked those qualities in her, but somehow this one only warmed her heart more, and she wondered how many other things she had yet to discover about Luce.

"Would I rather be getting a facial at a spa instead of being caked in mud after being kidnapped? Yes. The heart palpitations I've had this week have probably taken a good few years off my life. But the thing is… I don't *want* to go back to a time before I met you. Anxiety follows me everywhere, and I'm not sure that will ever change, but with you… with you, I can sometimes forget about it. With you, I never know what's coming, and you take me out of my own head. You make me feel like I'm more than just my illness. You… you understand me and accept me, even when I'm on the brink of a breakdown, and I don't get that with anyone else. Ever. I don't want to go home, Ophelia. I want to see this out with you. And we can wait until this is over or we can test Eilidh and her stupid fate, but if you're cursed, I'm happy to be cursed with you. We started this together and we'll end it that way, too. You're not getting rid of me."

Ophelia gulped, cupping Luce's jaw gently. It was hard as bone, a string pulled too tight, but her sincerity shone in her every feature, every word, and Ophelia had no choice but to believe her. "And you'd tell me if it got too much? If you needed to stop and go back?"

"I'd tell you," Luce agreed. "In fact, I think I have told you approximately three hundred times. It's a bit late to start taking notice of it now."

Ophelia let out a choked laugh. "I *do* want to kiss you. I just… I can't yet."

"Okay." Luce rose and offered out her hand. "Then let's go and visit Eilidh. I'd like to discuss some things with her."

"Please don't piss her off any more than she already is. We might be one step away from being smote by a lightning strike." Ophelia accepted her hand and remained close to Luce as they set off again. The slopes were steeper than ever as they ascended toward the peaks, and anticipation brimmed in her gut. They weren't far from High Mór and the lake now.

They weren't far from the place where all of this had begun.

Chapter Thirteen

L uce had never been more relieved than when she caught sight of the first flickering light. It glowed from the window of an old, crumbling cottage, wrapped up peacefully in the violet dusk. Just walking on a smooth dirt road flattened by the thick wheels of tractors was enough for her to let out a long sigh. The air up here was fresh and easy to breathe through, where it had felt loamy and oppressive for the past few days, as though she'd been sucking it in through a straw.

"Please tell me we're here."

Ophelia smiled and squeezed Luce's hand. "We're here."

The hamlet of High Mór was as quaint as Luce had expected, with an awful lot of farmland and not much else. Still, there was a post office on the corner and winter-wilted flowers hanging in baskets on the occasional signpost. The streetlights were few and far between, and most of the other crooked buildings were houses with fenced gardens. Luce tried to imagine what it all must have looked like over a hundred years ago, when Eilidh had been here — if the tale was true, that was. Probably not much different, minus the electricity.

Luce almost squealed when Ophelia led her to a B&B named the Macintosh Inn, fenced off from a field of horses who were being guided into their stalls for the night by a farmer with an unlit pipe drooping from his mouth. It still wasn't the spa-slash-mansion she'd been hoping for, but it would surely have a bed and a working shower and toilet. It was more than she'd had since leaving Enid's.

A bell tinkled above their heads as they stepped into the blissful, golden warmth of the inn. Nobody awaited them at the front desk, and Luce took the opportunity to collapse onto an old-fashioned white couch, only able to hope that her mud-covered clothes wouldn't dirty it. Ophelia, of course, drifted straight over to the photographs, from modern ones to black-and-white. Luce couldn't make out much more of them from her distance.

"How far is the lake from here?" Luce asked. She was already trying not to doze off in the sudden comfort.

"Not long," Ophelia murmured. "Half an hour at most." She traced her fingers across the glass frames, freezing when she reached a sign by the desk. "Oh my God. Look."

Luce couldn't read the swirly handwriting from here. She begrudgingly stood up and read the sign, gasping when the words sank in through the fog of exhaustion. *Home of Eilidh Macintosh.* "Does it just mean the village, or the actual house?"

"I don't know." Impatiently, Ophelia rang the small bell on the front desk, using so much force that it was at risk of breaking apart.

It summoned a woman who looked too young to be running a B&B in the middle of nowhere. She shuffled out of what must

Chapter Thirteen

have been a kitchen or dining room, her features terse. "All right, love. Heard you the first time. And the fifth."

"Sorry." Ophelia flushed.

The woman crossed her arms over her chest expectantly, looking them up and down with wariness sharpening her hazel irises. "Bloody hell. Did you get lost on your hike?"

Ophelia ignored her completely. "It says here that this is the home of Eilidh Macintosh. That's the same Eilidh who died in the lake not far from here?"

"Aye, the only Eilidh I know of." The woman nodded.

"Do you mean that she lived here in this house or just around the village?"

"We're named the Macintosh B&B." The woman said it as though the answer was obvious, tapping the name of the inn on one of the hand-drawn pamphlets. "This is Eilidh's home. It always has been."

"Oh my goodness." Ophelia brought a hand to her forehead, stunned.

"Does this mean we're going to become even more cursed if we sleep here?" Luce couldn't help but slump, disappointed. Eilidh was becoming quite an inconvenience in her life.

"What do you mean 'more cursed'?" the woman asked.

Ophelia swallowed. "It's just... well..."

"The curse isn't real," the woman continued before Ophelia could explain. She placed a hand on her hip as though the conversation was boring her. "I'm a Macintosh myself, and I've had no trouble finding a wife. We've been together eight years now. Besides, most people believe the curse only comes from the ring, and nobody's seen that since my bloody barmy nanny threw it into the lake decades ago."

Both Luce's and Ophelia's lips parted in surprise. She was

115

a descendant of Eilidh's. Eilidh was real. Luce hadn't really believed any of it until now.

"You're related to Eilidh?" Ophelia repeated.

The woman nodded slowly. "Yes, love. Correct. Are you all right? You look as though you've seen a ghost."

Maybe Ophelia had. Luce tried to see what she must be envisioning: a woman from over a century ago, her dark hair braided, her features pointy and well-structured, wearing a dress rather than the casual sweatshirt and jeans. Was this how Eilidh had looked before her death?

"It's just…" Ophelia cleared her throat. "I didn't know Eilidh had descendants around. I've been here before, but nobody ever told me."

"Right…" Eilidh's descendant raised an eyebrow. "Do you want a room or not?"

"No. I mean, yes, but…" Ophelia dug into the breast pocket of her shirt, hidden beneath her coat and jumper. Luce's nerves spiked. What was she doing? What if the woman wanted to keep the ring for herself? How was Ophelia going to lift the curse if she made it known that she'd stolen what was probably now a family heirloom?

Apparently, Ophelia shared none of the same concerns. She laid the ring on the desk, her fingertips stained red from the cold and her eyes glossy. "I have the ring. At least, I think I do. I found it in the lake where Eilidh was believed to have died with her husband."

Awe spread across the woman's features. She picked up the ring as though it were a delicate shard of glass, her eyes as wide as saucers. "This is it," she whispered. "My mum showed me photographs of it, but… we thought Nan had lost the ring when she threw it into the lake. Mum searched for it for ages afterward. Years. How long have you had it?"

Ophelia bowed her head, ashamed. "Three years."

The woman's brows knitted together. "So why am I only hearing about it now?"

"I'm an archaeologist. I recovered the ring for an exhibit down in Farnoch. I truly had no idea that anybody was looking for it. I was always told Eilidh was a legend, that nobody really knew if the story was true, but I found the ring while searching for fossils and... well, it cursed me."

The woman's eyes narrowed, and she clenched the ring in her palm. "Right, well... I think you'd both better come and sit down in the kitchen."

* * *

Ophelia warmed her hands around the delicate, floral-patterned teacup the woman — Iona, she had finally introduced herself as while boiling the kettle — had filled for her, the steam sticking to her chin. Across from her, Luce slumped in her own chair, her lids hooded and heavy with the same exhaustion Ophelia felt. It had been a long day, an even longer week, and now Ophelia didn't know if any of it would be worth it — for her, at least. Iona would no doubt want to keep the ring as a family heirloom, and she had every right to. But where would that leave Ophelia?

Where she already was, and had been for the past three years, probably. Alone, cursed, trapped. Her stomach wrenched with the thought as it never had before — because before, with the exception of Peter, the curse had only ruined tragic dates with strangers. Now, Luce was here, and she had wanted to kiss Ophelia, and Ophelia wanted to kiss her, and they couldn't.

Not unless Ophelia was ready to lose somebody else she cared for.

"So," Iona began with a sigh after dropping a sugar cube into her own tea. "You believe in the curse?"

Ophelia nodded and frowned. "Don't you?"

A shrug. "My nanny was always a little bit dramatic. When my mum told me the story of her throwing the ring into the lake because of a curse that had ruined her marriage, I just assumed she'd gone a bit loopy in her old age. It wasn't until I was older that I learned about Eilidh and the story of the ring, but even Mum didn't know if it was true or just something that had become part of the tale. We get guests asking about it, of course, but... well, I could only tell them what I'd been told: a vague story of us Macintosh women and our tragic love lives."

"You said you had a wife," Ophelia remembered. There had always been the second tale, the curse that followed Eilidh's family with or without the ring, but Iona had made it clear she didn't believe in it when they'd arrived. "The curse wasn't passed down to you."

"Nope. As far as I know, my mum was safe from it, too. She's been happily married to my dad for nigh on fifty years now. If the curse exists, maybe Nan was right. Maybe it's the ring." Her eyes fell warily to Eilidh's ring. It sat on the linen tablecloth in the center of the table, a midnight blue in the low light of the kitchen. "If that's the case, you can keep it well away from me."

"You don't want to keep it?" asked Luce, raising an eyebrow as she sipped her tea.

Iona shook her head. "And risk losing my wife and looking as sad and pathetic as you two? No, thanks. I'm not superstitious, but just the sight of it is giving me the heebie-jeebies."

"Thanks." Luce narrowed her eyes as though offended.

Ophelia, on the other hand, was inclined to agree with Iona. The ring had brought her nothing but bad luck, and she wouldn't wish it on anyone. "Still," she wondered aloud, "it's a big part of your family's legend. What will you do with it?"

Pensively, Iona tapped a long fingernail against her china teacup and weighed up the ring as though it were her hulking opponent in a wrestling match. "What did *you* intend to do with it?"

"I... I was hoping to take it back to the lake," Ophelia admitted feebly. The plan had sounded like a good one until now, sitting across from Eilidh's descendant. Now, she couldn't even trust that it would lift the curse. Leonard certainly hadn't been very sure. "Another archaeologist suggested that I'd be able to lift the curse if I returned it to Eilidh's resting place. I don't know how true it is...."

"It worked for Nan, I suppose," Iona said. "She met her second husband about a year after my grandad left her, which was when she also threw away the ring. They were together until Nan died — and even then, he followed her not long after. They're buried together, too."

Finally, a kernel of hope lifted in Ophelia's chest, and she allowed herself to feel it, to bask in it. "Really?" She couldn't conceal her excitement.

A smile spread across Iona's lips. She was all crooked teeth and laughter lines — miles friendlier than she'd appeared at the front desk not long ago. "Aye, really."

Ophelia tried to stifle her glee behind a sip of tea. "Wouldn't your mother want the ring, though?"

Iona sighed and crossed her legs, pushing her teacup away. "Honestly? It sounds like our family is better off without the ring — and so are you, apparently. If Eilidh's curse really exists, better we bury it with her."

"So... you wouldn't mind if I returned it to the lake?" Ophelia allowed herself to brighten then, her gaze meeting Luce's as she smiled. The curse could be left behind. Ophelia could believe in love again. She could move on. Maybe she could do it with Luce.

Luce beamed back at her, her eyes golden in the dim kitchen light — sunlight in the dead of winter, warm enough to thaw Ophelia's fear and dread. And Ophelia wondered for the first time if she'd been wrong about the curse all along, because it couldn't exist if it had brought Luce into her life. Luce could never be anything but sparkling good luck. If Ophelia was cursed, Luce was the opposite. She had been the opposite from the moment they'd met, even when angry and afraid and sharp-tempered. She was a fierce defiance against Eilidh's ring: a bright, fiery ruby against the dark sapphire.

She was Ophelia's gateway, her escape, from the walls that had been pressing in on her grieving heart for three years.

"No, I wouldn't mind." Iona reached out and placed her hand atop Ophelia's knuckles softly. Her attention fell to Luce, though. "We all deserve a proper chance at happiness, don't we? Looks like yours is sitting in front of you. Who am I to get in the way of that?"

Fire crept up Ophelia's cheeks, but she didn't have it in her to hide it. Luce's face turned just as rosy, her foot nudging Ophelia's shin gently beneath the table.

"Thank you," Ophelia said to Iona sincerely.

"I'll take you to the lake myself first thing tomorrow. How's that?" Iona released Ophelia's hand and sat back in her chair. "Besides, I want to know how you two met."

Luce rolled her eyes. "She stole my canoe."

"I *borrowed* it," Ophelia corrected, smirking at Luce. Her heart warmed, melted, working properly for the first time in a long time — and Ophelia found that she was no longer afraid of what that meant. The curse would be gone tomorrow, and even if it wasn't… Luce would still be here. She'd said as much today.

"She almost drowned me," Luce retorted, completely oblivious to Ophelia's gaze. It was also the first time Ophelia had seen Luce at ease. Her features weren't crinkled with worry, her smile not forced, her jaw not clenched.

Luce began to tell the story of how they'd met then, and Ophelia listened as though the story were another myth, another legend, just like Eilidh's. Only this one wasn't about a curse or death or unfaithfulness. This one was just a funny little tale of an unexpected adventure, one that had brought them both here, together, now.

Ophelia much preferred it, and she vowed then to hold on to it long after the ring sank to the bottom of the lake tomorrow. No matter what waited for her afterward, she wanted Luce with her.

Maybe now she would at least have a chance.

Chapter Fourteen

They walked down to the lake together, Luce and Ophelia hand in hand while Iona trailed behind with her wife, Cat. It was beautiful, a gleaming pearl tucked between the mountains and the overcast sky. Luce wouldn't have minded being laid to rest here herself, though under better circumstances than Eilidh's perhaps.

As they crunched their way to the gravelly lip of the lake's banks, Luce squeezed Ophelia's hand, the wind whipping through their hair and tangling their dark-brown and rusty-golden strands into knots. "Are you ready?"

Ophelia nodded and forced a smile, her chest rising and falling with a deep breath. "I am."

Luce sucked in the sharp air, too, feeling refreshed and relaxed for the first time in days. Years, even. The breeze seemed to blow away the fog and the fear, though she knew these temporary reprieves never lasted forever. For a moment, though, it felt like they could, and she relished every second that passed easily, every breath that wasn't forced, every movement that wasn't unsteady. If she could survive the last few days in the Scottish Highlands, she could survive anything her body and mind put her through next.

Worrying at her lip, Ophelia pulled the ring out from her coat pocket and balanced it in her palm. Iona peered over her shoulder, and Luce couldn't help but whisper a silent goodbye to it. Cursed or not, it had gotten them here, together. It had brought Ophelia hurtling headfirst into Luce's life. Luce wouldn't wish to change that.

After a moment of stillness, Ophelia's fingers curled around the ring and she steeled herself again. Luce waited for her to throw it into the lake — but she didn't. She looked at Luce through glossy, pale eyes and dark lashes and tugged her closer.

"I don't know if I was ever cursed or not, but I... I know that *we* weren't. If anything, you were a blessing, Luce. The curse could never touch you. I'm not afraid of that anymore."

Luce's lips parted with a reply — what, she didn't know — but it drifted away as Ophelia kissed her, her hands twining through Luce's knotty hair, her flesh warm, their bodies flush together. Luce's knees wobbled, her stomach swooping with surprise, with warmth, and she kissed back until she ached.

And then Iona's feigned gagging noise broke the sparks building between them. Luce pulled away with a coy smile, blood pumping in her ears and heat prickling across her face. She'd never let herself be vulnerable with anybody before. She'd never let go of her worries and just taken what she wanted.

But with Ophelia, she wanted too much to stop herself. Ophelia had seen her at her worst and had still made Luce feel understood, supported. There was nothing left to be afraid of with her, no part of her that could be any more terrible than what they'd already endured. Now Ophelia could discover Luce's better parts — and there *were* better parts. Luce was more than just the gloomy, volatile ball of anxiety and depression she sometimes felt like. She'd discovered that, too, this week, or had at least been reminded of it.

Ophelia glanced down at the ring again and, closing her eyes, threw it into the lake. It landed with a plop, disrupting the smooth surface of the water, sending a ripple lapping out onto the banks. "Maybe if it's ever found again, its owner will have better luck than the rest of us — like we did."

Luce smiled and snaked her arm around Ophelia's waist. Ophelia tucked her head into the crook of Luce's neck, the smell of vanilla soap courtesy of Iona wafting around them. "I'm certain they will," Luce whispered.

They stayed that way for a while, wondering whether Eilidh was close, whether there was anything left of her here at all, or whether it was all gone now, another story that would become a legend and then a myth and then a cautionary tale until, eventually, she was forgotten completely.

It would always feel real to Luce — but never as real as Ophelia and her touch and her laugh and her comfort. Eilidh was a ghost. For a while, Luce had felt like one, too, always focused on work so that she wouldn't have to face the things inside of her.

But she didn't feel like that now. This lake was a reminder that Luce was alive, no matter how difficult it was sometimes. She was alive, and she was ready to create stories of her own — with Ophelia.

And they'd already started.

Chapter Fifteen

◈

J olting to a stop in the carpark of Alasdair Ridge was a
strange feeling. Ophelia felt untethered without the ring,
as though she were a helium balloon roaming the skies.
It was terrifying and liberating, but sad, too. She wished that
Peter were still here, wished that she could talk to him about it
without it changing her time with Luce.

Perhaps it was time to just be content with what was. She
could miss Peter and want Luce at the same time, couldn't she?
Her feelings for one didn't negate her feelings for the other.
Besides, this was why she'd been so desperate to get rid of the
curse: to love again. Only then such a thing had felt so distant,
so unreachable. Now Luce was here, and Ophelia was here,
and the ring wasn't, and her nerves jangled over what would
come next.

"Thank you, Iona," Ophelia said finally, slipping off her
seatbelt. Iona had driven them home — in a tractor that
smelled like manure, that was, borrowed from Iona's wife. "For
everything. I'm so glad I got to meet you."

"And I you," Iona agreed, resting her elbows against the steering wheel. "I told my mum all about it this morning. She was so glad to hear that all of this curse malarkey could finally be put to bed. What about you? Do you feel any different?"

Ophelia couldn't help but glance at Luce, the corner of her mouth quirking into a smile. "I do."

Luce took her hand and squeezed gently. "As much as I've enjoyed meeting you, Iona, I really just want to go and get my pajamas on. Nice, clean pajamas that smell like my own detergent. Oh my God, and I never have to touch mud again. Ever. I can shower every night and wee on an actual toilet instead of a bush, and..." The excited rambling trailed away with Luce as she hopped out of the tractor and wandered toward the cabins, barely sparing either of them a wave.

"Bye, then," Iona mumbled.

With a snort, Ophelia shook her head. She wondered if she and Luce would still be the same now that they weren't just trying to survive in the wilderness. There were so many things about Luce that Ophelia didn't know, and they didn't live all that close by, either. Ophelia wasn't afraid, though. If they were meant to be — and, after all they'd endured, Ophelia believed they were — they'd make it work.

"What's next for you two, then?" Iona asked, motioning her head toward Luce's retreating form. "Do you think she's 'the One'? Worth the efforts you went through to get Eilidh's ring back to the lake?"

The butterflies fluttering around Ophelia's stomach were answer enough, but she shrugged in an effort to remain nonchalant. They'd only known each other for a few days, after all. "I don't know yet. But I'm looking forward to finding out."

126

Iona smirked knowingly. "You'll have to visit us in High Mór again."

"If I'd have known it was accessible by tractor rather than only on foot, I would have found you all sooner."

"Well, part of the fun is the journey up there. That's what I always say to my guests, anyway. They usually curse me out, mind, since they've just hiked up a mountain for three days."

Ophelia chuckled again, searching for some sort of hint of Eilidh in Iona. Perhaps they might have shared the same pointy nose or upturned eyes, but Ophelia found that she was beginning to care less and less. Iona wasn't Eilidh. She'd broken the cycle of bad luck, just like her mother, and she wasn't destined for the same tragedies. Ophelia liked that about her more than any relation she shared with a legendary ancestor.

"Well, until next time, then." Ophelia slid across the bench and used the door handle as support as she climbed out of the tractor.

"Aye. Take care, Ophelia." Iona nodded and waved as Ophelia shut the door, and then the tractor whirred to life again, its mammoth tires crushing dirt and gravel as she drove away, leaving a foul stench in her wake. A few people around the camp had stopped to see the spectacle, but Ophelia ignored them all as she skipped cheerily toward the cabins. She glanced around, unsure of which was Luce's until she appeared on the doorstep of one in the corner.

"Hurry up," she scolded. "I'm freezing."

"And as patient as ever, I see," Ophelia retorted, rushing into the cabin. It was warm and carried the smell of wood and musk, comforting.

"I was just informed that a search party had been sent out for me after the canoe incident. Naturally, I told them that I was kidnapped by a madwoman, so don't be surprised if the police come knocking." Luce swung the door shut and kicked off her boots — the ones loaned to her by Enid, along with the lost belongings she'd have to be reimbursed for now. That part of their saga felt eons ago.

"I'm sure they will either way," Ophelia replied, shucking off her raincoat. "I did steal an ancient artifact."

"What will you tell the museum?"

Ophelia shrugged, untying the laces of her boots slowly. "The truth, I suppose. Perhaps if I explain it to Morag, the owner, she'll understand."

"You could lie. Say that Hector stole the ring. Besides, you have a defense lawyer on your side. I'm sure I can find a way to get you out of charges."

She couldn't help but smirk, straightening and pulling Luce in by the waist so that their soft bellies pressed together and their faces were inches apart. "Last I heard, my lawyer was threatening to sue me."

"Well," Luce breathed, her nose grazing Ophelia's and her lips parting hungrily. "My lawsuit probably wouldn't have held up in court, given the unprofessional nature of our relationship."

Warmth unfurled in Ophelia's stomach, her heart beating so fast that she worried Luce would feel it. *Relationship.* She'd wondered if Luce would change her mind now they were home, back to reality, but she was still here, inches away. Ophelia couldn't help herself. She pressed her lips to Luce's, her fingers tucking strands of brown hair behind Luce's ear.

"I should talk to Morag before I get arrested," she whispered, the tug of the outside world calling for her. It left anxiety spiraling in her gut. She'd been joking earlier, but what if Morag *did* press charges? What if Ophelia had ruined her life because of Eilidh's ring?

"You're not going to get arrested." Luce kissed Ophelia's forehead so delicately that Ophelia's knees went weak. "It will be fine. I'm sure of it."

"Is that your professional opinion?"

"Yes." Luce wandered into the small, rustic kitchen and filled the kettle. "Morag can wait a few more hours."

Ophelia worried at her lip. "Luce…"

"Hmm?" Luce asked distractedly, flicking on the switch and pulling out two mugs. The water began to boil, filling the quiet between them.

Perhaps Ophelia should have let her questions die there with the bubbling of the kettle and the banging of the cupboard doors. Perhaps she should have washed down her unease with her tea and let it lie there, silent and heavy. But she wasn't that sort of person, and she had to know what Luce was thinking, what she wanted. "What about us?"

Luce's motions slowed and then, as she turned, stopped completely. She narrowed her eyes. "What *about* us?"

"Well…" Ophelia gulped. "*Is* there an 'us'? Do you want there to be? Because you live in Manchester and I live here, and… well, we barely know each other, really."

It wasn't the truth. Ophelia did know Luce, in all the ways that mattered. She knew that when she felt anxious, a little bit like now, her jaw clenched and her posture stiffened, and she remained catatonically still unless in bed. She knew that Luce slept curled up on her right side, her knees tucked to her chest. She knew that Luce liked to drink coffee in the morning but tea at night. She knew that peppermint oil helped her nervous stomach, and she knew that she was braver than she knew. She knew that before Luce kissed her she licked her lips, and

129

no matter how badly she wanted to give up when things got difficult, she never did.

Ophelia knew all of these things about Luce, and they felt so personal, so important, that it hadn't occurred to her how easy it would be to become strangers again until now.

"Are you... are you saying that you don't want to keep this going once I leave?"

Ophelia's brows furrowed as she inched toward Luce in the kitchen. "*No*. No, I'm saying the opposite. I just wasn't sure where *you* wanted to leave us. I don't want to assume we're something more than we are."

"Well..." Luce began to fidget with the teaspoons in the kitchen drawer. "I don't know, honestly. You're right: it's only been a few days, and I live so far away. Maybe it would be silly to jump into something so complicated."

"Oh." Ophelia's hope wilted, her chest aching. She'd hoped that Luce — practical, intelligent Luce — would give her the reassurance she needed, would give her a solution to whatever problems lay ahead. "I suppose you're right."

"It's just... well, distance aside, I'm not that great at relationships. It takes so much energy for me just to survive the day sometimes. I'm not sure I'd be the sort of partner you deserve." Luce's eyes gleamed with tears. She turned around, clutching the countertop tightly enough that her knuckles turned white. She heaved a deep breath and poured the tea, her hands unsteady and almost spilling the water everywhere.

Ophelia didn't know what to say. Was Luce telling her that she didn't want to be with her, or was pushing Ophelia away another symptom of her anxiety?

"You know I'd be patient," Ophelia murmured gently. "I understand that you struggle, but that doesn't mean you have to spend your life alone, Luce. Perhaps it would be easier if you had somebody to lean on."

"You say that now, but it's not reality. I've tried relationships before. It doesn't work. People get bored of this eventually: canceled plans and long work hours and grinding your teeth through the night. Nobody wants to deal with that, do they?"

Ophelia stepped slowly to Luce's side, brushing her mussed hair from her shoulder so that she could see her face properly. Luce's eyes were cast down, her trembling lips pressed into a thin line. Maybe it wasn't Ophelia who needed the reassurance, she realized. Maybe it was Luce.

"I recall that you didn't want to deal with me or the curse at first, either. And then you got me to High Mór and you helped me figure it all out, and I couldn't have done it without you in the end." Ophelia wished Luce would look at her, but she didn't, so Ophelia spoke to her profile desperately. "I'd never see your anxiety as a reason not to try with you. We can take it at your speed if you're afraid and work the rest out as we go, but if you like me the way I like you… I don't want it to end yet. I meant what I said at the lake this morning. You were never part of the curse. You were the *opposite* of the curse, Luce, and I'm not ready to let you go. Not unless you want me to."

Finally, Luce lifted her focus, though she stared at the kitchen tiles rather than Ophelia. "I don't want you to," she admitted. "I just wish I could be different for you."

"I don't." Ophelia shook her head and tilted Luce's chin toward her so that Luce would know she meant it. "I like you, and an illness that goes beyond your control isn't going to change that. It's not a character flaw, Luce, and it's not a burden to me. It's just another mountain we'll climb together."

A tear rolled down Luce's cheek. "You always know the right

things to say."

"I know," Ophelia teased. "It's one of the many reasons I would make quite a good girlfriend. Just saying."

Something between a laugh and a sob fell from Luce as she pulled Ophelia in, and then they were kissing again, lips salty with Luce's tears, and Ophelia knew she had meant every word she'd said. Nothing meant to end could feel this good, and Ophelia would hold on to it just to prove it. She wanted Luce — whether she was covered in mud or unable to sleep or doubting herself or miles and miles away in Manchester, Ophelia wanted her.

"I hope we can still kiss when I'm behind bars," Ophelia whispered.

Luce only rolled her eyes and pressed her forehead to Ophelia's. "You're *not* getting arrested, Ophelia. They'll have to go through me first."

Despite her fears, Ophelia would have quite liked to see such a thing.

* * *

Reluctantly, Ophelia stepped into the museum. It was deserted, though in better shape than when Ophelia had left it. The shattered glass had been cleared from the floor, the podium that had once displayed Eilidh's ring now empty.

"Morag?" Ophelia called, her voice echoing around the cold space. The older woman was usually hovering around somewhere, but there were no visitors to attend to today, and she seemed to have given up hope that there would be. "Morag, are you here?"

The shuffling of feet approached from the back corridor. A

moment later, Morag appeared, her face crinkled in confusion. When she took Ophelia in, shock crossed her features and her hand rose to her chest. "Oh, thank goodness! You're back! What happened to you?"

Ophelia was pulled into a hug before she could protest. Morag patted her shoulder lovingly, smelling of the lemony washing-up liquid in the kitchen and the flowery perfumes that the soap shop sold next door. Ophelia, on the other hand, still smelled like horse poo and mud. She hadn't even bothered to go home and change her clothes before coming here, too nervous to waste more time putting it off.

"I was ever so worried about you, lovely."

She didn't know, then, that her employee was a thief. "Morag, there's something I need to talk to you about…"

"Not before I put the kettle on, there isn't!" Morag batted Ophelia's protests away and went back into the corridor. Ophelia had no choice but to follow her sheepishly into the kitchen. "Honestly, when that fancy professor of yours turned up and told me what had happened, I was beside myself!"

"What?" Ophelia's brows furrowed in surprise. "What professor?" She knew only one — but why would Leonard come back to the museum?

"That dashing silver fox who used to teach you!" Morag pulled two mugs from the cupboard and flicked the kettle on. "He explained everything."

Ophelia doubted that. "What, exactly, did he say?"

"That you were forced to give Eilidh's ring to an awful thief and take him to the lake for more sapphires! I mean, it's like something out of a book, isn't it? I'm just so glad you weren't hurt."

"Morag…" Ophelia stuttered, lost for words. Leonard had

tried to clear Ophelia's blame. He should have gone straight home to his family with Hector's money, but he'd come back for Ophelia's sake. It didn't make sense — and she couldn't let her responsibility for the theft of Eilidh's ring be wiped clean. The guilt gnawed at her too much for that. "I wish Leonard's story was true, but that isn't quite the way it happened."

Morag frowned. "What do you mean?"

Ophelia steeled herself, biting down on her lip as though the pain might help her through it. "It was me who stole the ring. There was a thief here for it, yes, but... when I saw that they'd broken the display, I got it before they could."

"All right. So where is it now?"

"In the lake where I found it, up near High Mór."

Morag's hand fell to her hip, her posture stiffening. "Why didn't you bring it back *here*?"

"Because..." Ophelia closed her eyes before they could produce tears. She didn't deserve sympathy for this. What she'd done was wrong, no matter how necessary it had felt, and Morag would be right to take her straight to the police. "The ring was cursed, and I needed to get rid of it. I'm so sorry, Morag. I know how important the exhibit was. But the ring has only ever caused suffering, and it needed to be returned to a place where it couldn't keep hurting people."

Moments passed between them, nothing to fill them but the burbling kettle. Morag stared blankly as though she hadn't heard Ophelia's words at all. "So what you're telling me," she said slowly, finally, "is that you took the ring because of the curse?"

Ophelia bowed her head in shame. "Yes."

"Why did you never mention it before, then? If you thought you were cursed, you know I would have helped you."

She didn't deserve Morag's soft questioning. She deserved anger and accusation, not this quiet sense of understanding. "I was... I was ashamed. After losing Peter, I didn't know what to do. And then when I tried to date again, I began to notice a pattern, and I was so certain it was the ring that had caused me all of the heartache — even Peter's death. I didn't even plan to do anything about it, not until Leonard and Hector showed up and broke through the display. I didn't think after that; I just ran. I knew if they got to the ring first, I'd never have a chance at being free from the curse. It was wrong, Morag, and I'm so sorry."

But she wasn't. Not really. No matter what happened now, she'd met Luce and Iona and she'd lifted the curse. She wouldn't have changed that for anything. Maybe that made her awful and selfish, but maybe she didn't really care anymore. Three years spent blaming herself for her fiancé's death, and she could finally breathe again.

Morag only blinked, her features excruciatingly blank. Ophelia frowned and continued. "I met a descendant of Eilidh's in High Mór. I asked her if she wanted to keep the ring. It wasn't ever mine to dispose of, after all, and I know that now. But Iona agreed that the ring should be laid to rest with Eilidh, and so we threw it in the lake together." She paused, waiting for a reaction. Morag gave none. "Please say something, Morag. I know you must feel betrayed and furious, and you have every right to be, but—"

"Oh, sweetheart." Morag softened, the corners of her eyes crinkling with what looked like understanding. Ophelia could only hope it was understanding. "I'm not furious at all. I had no idea that the ring had had such an effect on you. I only wish you would have told me about it. I would have helped you, you know."

"But… everybody comes to visit Eilidh's ring. It was the most important exhibit in the museum."

"It wasn't worth all of the upset you've been through since finding it." Morag placed her hands on Ophelia's shoulders and squeezed. "You were right to take it to Eilidh's family, and if they decided it was best to let the ring go, there's nothing I could have said to change it. This isn't the sort of museum that steals from its own people, Ophelia, and it never has been. As long as the ring is where it should be now, that's all that matters. Besides, you look like you've been through hell and back. Whose clothes are these?"

She tugged at the hem of the knitted jumper Enid had loaned Ophelia, and Ophelia laughed through her tears. "They belonged to a friend we met along the way."

Morag raised a curious eyebrow. "'We'?"

"Oh, yes… there's more to the story. I met someone special on my way to the lake.…" Ophelia perched on the kitchen counter and began her story. Morag listened intently, stirring milk and sugar into the mugs of tea and *ooh*ing and *aah*ing in all the right places. And as Ophelia spoke about her adventure with Luce, she couldn't help but smile. No matter the grave reasons that had driven her to take the ring home, she had made heartwarming, hilarious memories with a woman she was falling for — and that was something she would hold close to her heart for the rest of her life, just as she did with her memories of Peter.

In the end, the journey hadn't been about Eilidh's ring at all. It had been about Luce. Ophelia knew that now more than ever.

Epilogue

⁓◦◦◦⁓

fter an afternoon of explaining her whereabouts over
the past few days to Alex, the receptionist at Alasdair
Ridge, and soaking away all the grime and anxiety
in the small bathtub in her room, Luce woke up feeling
surprisingly refreshed — though perhaps a little tired — the
following morning. She'd even managed to call Juliet from
Alex's phone to give her an earful about sending her here instead
of a spa, which had left her feeling much more like herself again.

After a relaxing morning trying and failing to get a signal
on her old-fashioned television and eating all of the toast and
butter she could stomach, she found herself already missing
Ophelia. Embarrassing, perhaps, but true. So Luce decided to
reacquaint herself with her car and head into Farnoch to find
her. It was a small village of waterwheels and charity shops
— and beyond that a lot of cows. Luce scowled at them as she
drove by, remembering her run-in with the Highland cow that
had chased her across the fields a few days ago. Thank God
these ones were all fenced up.

She found Farnoch's museum beside a cottage that sold handmade soaps and wafted the scent of sweet roses as Luce walked past. Before heading into the museum, though, she crossed the road and bought two hot chocolates to go, as well as a couple of blueberry muffins. After starving and freezing in the Highlands for three days, she would never take cake and hot drinks for granted again.

The museum was as quiet as the rest of the village, and just as rustic inside. It was almost like stepping into somebody's home, only the furniture had been swapped for exhibits protected by glass. She hovered over the museum label about Eilidh for a few minutes, reading the story she now knew was true and noting the empty space where the ring should have been.

"Find something interesting?" a musical voice questioned behind her.

Luce smiled and turned around, offering out one of the hot chocolates. "I've heard more interesting stories."

"Is that right?" Ophelia arched an eyebrow. She was glowing today, in fresh, clean clothes. It was odd and disconcerting seeing her so put-together in a tweed dress and white blouse, almost as though she had belonged in the mountains and now she was just playing dress-up. Still, she was more beautiful than ever, and Luce's heart leaped into her throat as though confirming everything they'd shared still existed, still mattered, even if their adventure had come to its close.

Luce nodded and couldn't help but peck Ophelia on the lips. It felt different, perhaps more real, because they were somewhere safe and warm, somewhere where they were just themselves, without the added stress of trying to survive.

It felt easier.

"I wasn't expecting to see you today. I thought you'd have

gone straight home and never come back," Ophelia admitted quietly.

"You think I'd leave without a goodbye?" Luce frowned and placed down her cup.

Alarmed, Ophelia picked it straight back up. "Be careful of the exhibits, Luce. I've already made enough of a mess in here this week."

Luce's nose wrinkled with endearment. Ophelia was still so Ophelia, and yet somehow completely new. There were so many more things to adore about her here, and still so many things to learn about her. "I can't help but notice that you haven't been arrested yet."

"Well, Morag was actually very understanding of it all, which was more than I deserved. Looks like I'm staying out of prison... for now."

"Always a relief," Luce agreed, leaning against the front desk as she sipped her hot chocolate. "I was already planning around the visiting hours."

"What about you?" Ophelia bowed her head and fiddled with a button on her dress absently. "How long do I have you for before you go home?"

"Well, I have three years' worth of holidays to use up at work. I suppose I could stick around for a week or so, maybe. If you'd like me to."

Her features brightened, blue eyes sparkling as she lifted her gaze. "Really?"

Luce couldn't help but grin so widely that it made her cheeks ache. The thought of being away from home for another week still left anxiety dancing in her stomach, but that was overpowered by the warmth she felt for Ophelia. She would always struggle, always wish all of those chemicals rushing around inside her brain were built differently, but that didn't mean she couldn't choose happiness when it passed her by. And now happiness was here, staring her in the face, and Luce wasn't ready to let it go yet.

"As long as we stay clear of mud, cows, cursed rings, and canoes. Also, no more weeing in bushes."

"These all sound like reasonable requests." Ophelia tugged Luce closer by the wrists, brushing Luce's hair from her eyes. "I'm sure we can find something to do that doesn't involve weeing in bushes. In fact, I can think of a few things."

Ophelia pressed her lips to Luce's, kissing soft and slow, as though they had all the time in the world. Maybe they did. Luce let herself hope that perhaps they did. She tasted of mint and smelled like lavender, her cheeks rosy, her eyelashes fluttering, and Luce soaked up every ounce of sunlight Ophelia radiated, grateful just to be so close to her.

She didn't know what would happen next week, or even tomorrow, but she knew that she was here, now, with a woman who had carried her through rain and tears and anger and anxiety and, above all of that, joy. For once, Luce was okay with not having a plan. She was okay with the fear of not knowing.

She was okay because she'd met Ophelia.

About the Author

Bryony Rosehurst is a British romance author dedicated to telling diverse stories of love and happily ever afters — and perhaps a little bit of angst sprinkled in for good measure. You can usually find her painting (badly), photographing new cities (occasionally), or wishing for autumn (always). Chat with her on Twitter: @BryonyRosehurst.

Printed in Great Britain
by Amazon

22638250R00088